Disciplined by the Dom

A Club Volare Novel

Chloe Cox

DEDICATION

To anyone who ever gave me a book, even if it was just to get me to be quiet.

CONTENTS

Just a Quick Note...

Dear Reader,

Disciplined by the Dom took me completely by surprise. Actually, to be specific, Jake took me completely by surprise. I realized in the middle of the first draft that he had become an amalgamation of a few people I've known and admired for their quiet tenacity. The one thing that kept coming back to me was that this was a guy who tried his hardest to be his best, even when no one was watching, and even when he didn't think anyone should believe in him. It made me love him, a little bit. ;)

So this book became about the leaps of faith that make up a relationship—the bravery involved, the risks people take, the wounds they accept, and ultimately the ways they choose to love each other. This one really got to me. I hope it gets to you, too. :)

Oh, and since I apparently can't stop myself from doing this (!), this one also has at least one thing that you should *not* try at home without some training and research first. (Chapters 20-21.) If you're interested, there are plenty of websites out there, so definitely do your homework first. (Jake and Catie are on the riskier end of the spectrum here, though they do take precautions.)

Wishing you lots of love and happiness,
Chloe

Those who fly...

chapter 1

Catie Roberts looked nervously over her shoulder, lit a match, and set fire to the folder containing every last shred of her personal information. Then she thought about all the things that had led her to this awful moment.

Catie was in the private office of one Lola Theroux, Mistress of the secretive society, Club Volare, and someone who'd been really nice to her. And Catie was setting fires, fires that would burn away all the evidence that Catie was not who she claimed to be, that she was lying to everyone, that she was here not to learn about BDSM or herself, but that instead, she was here to betray them all.

It made her want to cry. Instead she reminded herself that she had to be ruthless, and watched the flames lick their way up the manila folder.

You have no one else, Catie. It's up to you.

She gritted her teeth and thought about the day this all started—the worst day of her life. As the fire grew, she kept one eye on the door, terrified of being found out.

A minute later, that door would open, and Catie Roberts would be sure that everything was coming to an end.

A minute after that, and she'd be naked.

The worst day of her life, the day that would, somehow, through a series of unpredictable twists and turns, lead to Catie naked and kneeling before a Dom in the New York offices of Club Volare, had started with a break up.

Catie had spent all morning learning lines from Brian's latest script so she could help him prepare for his audition, but he hadn't come over to run a scene. He'd come over to dump her.

"No," Catie had said.

"'No?'" Brian looked confused. "You can't just say no."

Catie rolled and unrolled the untried script in her hands, trying not to let her anxiety show. Brian was just standing there, with his hair artfully tussled into a studied bedhead look, his two-day scruff carefully trimmed, giving her that *look*, that look that a man will give a woman that says he's just waiting for her to see logic. It was so infuriating it made it hard to think. Of course, she couldn't just say no to a break up. That wasn't the point.

"It's not fair," she tried to explain.

Brian rubbed the back of his neck and looked at

the floor. "Look, Catie, you're a great girl—"

"Don't say that," she said, feeling the tears begin to well up. She'd be so upset if she cried. "That makes it sound like..."

But she couldn't continue. All at once, the reality of the situation hit her: his shifting body language, the way he kept moving towards the door, the way he wouldn't look her in the eye. There was no point. Maybe there'd never been a point. Why did it hurt so much, then? If they weren't supposed to be together? If it was such a bad match? Even Catie couldn't deny that maybe they didn't quite fit. They spent a lot of time clarifying the things they said to each other, compromising on movies, laughing at different times. So why did she care? Why had she put so much into it? Why was her heart broken?

"It's just that people are supposed to be there for you when you're there for them," she whispered.

Brian looked uncomfortable, but he didn't look sorry. He said, "I gotta go, Catie."

And then he was gone. Her apartment felt empty. Her roommate was on a paid junket in Vegas, modeling...something. It seemed like the perfect time to eat ice cream and feel sorry for herself. She grabbed a pint of *dulce de leche* and snuggled into the corner of the couch, remote and phone within easy reach.

Catie knew she shouldn't call her father. She knew he probably wouldn't talk to her about her emotional problems, that he'd probably just silently wait her out until he could bring up "business"—the management of the trust fund her grandfather had left her, which he controlled until she turned twenty-five. That's if he even picked up. He hadn't answered her calls in at least a week, but Catie kept trying, just like she tried now, even though she knew from experience that her father's silence was likely to leave her feeling even worse. It was like a scab she couldn't help picking at. Part of her dreaded her twenty-fifth birthday because she wondered if they'd have anything to talk about at all after that.

Her twenty-fifth was so close. Just a few months. That sealed it: she called her dad.

He didn't pick up.

This was, in a way, almost better. Catie could pretend the conversation would have gone the way it did in her fantasies, with her dad breaking his usually stoic countenance to give her some gruff but wise advice, the kind of thing that would let her know he'd always been listening, even when it hadn't seemed like it. Like the way it would go in a movie.

But then her phone rang. It wasn't her dad; it was Mr. Everett, their family lawyer.

Catie listened intently, hearing the words, but not quite putting it all together.

"What do you mean 'he's gone?'" she asked.

"He's left, Catie," Mr. Everett said. He sounded tired. "He cleaned out everything and left. Apparently, he ran away with a married real estate agent in his office. He did it while I was on vacation."

"But I don't understand."

"He cleaned out nearly everything, Catie. Including your trust."

Again, Catie heard the words. She knew what

they all meant individually. She understood, on some intellectual level. But it all felt unreal. Like everything was underwater, in slow motion. Dulled.

"But he's ok?"

"As far as I know."

"Did he leave a note?" she asked. Her voice sounded sedated.

"He left one for me."

"Oh. Ok."

What was maybe most surprising was the total lack of surprise. Catie had always told herself that her dad's reticence wasn't personal, that that was just his way. That they might not get along, but they were still family. They still loved each other, could still rely on each other. Right? Of course, she'd always wondered how things might have been different if her mom had survived. Would they have been close? Would her grandmother have wanted to be part of their lives? Catie didn't really remember her mother as a person. She just remembered the smell of lavender lotion, and the feeling that she was loved and cared for wrapping around her like a warm blanket.

There was a long pause. Catie thought she could almost hear Mr. Everett working himself up to what came next.

"We have to talk about your grandmother," he said.

And that was how Catie found herself making the trip out to Ridge Hill again. It was different in the middle of a weekday instead of on a Sunday morning. She was used to going on Sundays. Never missed one. Wasn't going to miss this Sunday, either. She wasn't sure exactly what she thought she was going to accomplish—maybe talk to the nurses? Find out if it was possible for her Nana to come live with her?

Even as Catie's brain fizzed and sparked, trying to come up an idea—*any* idea—part of her knew it was hopeless. Her grandmother was slowly dying out there, and it had apparently been Catie's trust that paid for her care. Catie didn't mind that part, except that now it was gone.

There was an old woman with tangled white hair and dirt on her face on Catie's bus, muttering angrily to herself. Normally the sight of a mentally ill old woman with no one to take care of her would have just made Catie sad. Today, it made her crazy with fear. Nana was all the family Catie had. She was all she had left of her mom. She *couldn't* end up somewhere terrible.

When she got to Ridge Hill, her Nana was parked by a window, staring out at the street with glazed-over eyes. Catie had forgotten to bring her usual See's Candies.

"Nana?"

Her grandmother didn't answer. Catie pulled up a chair and just started talking. She hadn't really meant to do that. She'd come to see her grandmother with the intention of being strong and reassuring, but as soon as she sat down, it all just came pouring out.

"Nana, it's five thousand a month here," she finished, searching for one of the tissue boxes that were always nearby. "I don't know if I can pay that."

But she did know. Catie didn't even make five

thousand dollars a month between her sparse acting gigs and picking up various waitressing shifts. She'd never wanted her friends to know that she was actually a spoiled little rich girl, and she hadn't wanted to grow dependent on her trust fund—except now that it was gone, she realized how just the knowledge that it was there had made her life immeasurably easier. Now that it wasn't, the anxiety descended upon her like an ominous fog. She was overwhelmed by it.

Catie was choking on it when her grandmother spoke.

"You look like your father," Nana said, eyes focusing in a moment of lucidity. "You could charm your way into anything. People like to trust you."

Nana tried shaking her finger, and Catie knew she was about to get another lecture on what a scoundrel her dad was—a lecture she no longer needed. Catie told her grandmother that it would all be ok, even though she'd felt bad for lying, and soon after she took the bus home, wanting to just crawl into bed and go to sleep. But her grandmother's words wouldn't let her. They kept bouncing around inside her head, crashing into thoughts and memories and the random things Catie knew from the weird club jobs she worked, growing bigger and bigger, until finally Catie had an idea.

It was a terrible idea. But it was her only idea. There was one thing Catie knew, the one secret of value that she had. One thing she knew about because sometimes it was her job to get rich, famous men really drunk. And one place where she knew she could sell that secret, because she'd sold them gossip before.

Sizzle. Biggest gossip rag on the market. One of the only magazines that could still afford to stay in print.

She showed up unannounced, and her exchange with a man called Brazzer had been brief. He hadn't had much time for her, chewing and smacking his bubble gum while he looked through emails. "Nothing up front," he'd said. "Bring me some dirt good enough to print, I'll pay you cash."

And that was how Catie ended up in Mistress Lola's office at Club Volare NY, pretending to be a BDSM novice under an assumed name, destroying the employment documents she'd stupidly filled out with her real social security number.

"Moron," Catie muttered to herself. She'd thought to open the window while she burned away the evidence, but she hadn't made sure there was something to catch the ash or burning bits of paper. She should have emptied the trashcan. That would have been smart. But as it was, now she had about ten seconds to find somewhere to put the flaming folder.

Getting caught setting fire to things would *not* help with her already precarious position at the club. She'd been too petrified, so far, to choose a Dom as a trainer, and had instead fallen into the familiar patterns of stuff she knew: waitressing, hostessing, generally being charming. Never venturing into any of the novice classes, never learning the kinds of stuff she needed to learn. Lola had finally suggested—insisted, really—that Catie make her role at the club official, with official employment records and everything. Something about the way Lola had looked at her made Catie think that the red-haired Mistress was slightly suspicious, like there was an unstated concern about what Catie was doing, exactly, if she wasn't going to choose a trainer and commit to Volare instruction. Which had made Catie feel like crap; she *liked* Lola. Lola was a good person.

Be ruthless!

It wasn't that she didn't *want* to learn submission at the hands of a Dom. She actually dreamed about exactly that. She'd just never found the right partner. Brian had looked terrified whenever she'd brought it up, so eventually she'd just stopped. Picking a trainer at Club Volare should have been like picking a birthday present. But as it turned out, there was only really one Dom she wanted. Jake.

Jake, the mystery man. The sexy professor type, except there was something else about him, something remote and refined. The man was tall, brooding, and severe, with a streak of early silver on one side of his head, a narrow waist, a broad chest, thick arms, and absolutely no interest in her. As much as she tried to avoid noticing him, it was impossible not to notice that he studiously avoided her, too, even when he tended bar while she hung out in the lounge.

And because she wanted him so much, she couldn't trust herself. Catie was a good actress, but she had no illusions. She'd never win an Oscar, and she was terrified of being exposed. Because while she was here under false pretenses, with the intention to betray all of these people, Club Volare was still the closest she'd come in a long time to feeling like she had a family. And she spent so much energy keeping up this front and trying to make notes about all the stuff that she saw and basically lying, all the time, to everybody, that she wasn't at all certain that she'd be able to maintain her facade while in the throes of…whatever it was Jake might do to her.

She shivered. Just the thought of him…

"Ow!"

She'd waited too long, and now she was holding a burning ember between her fingers. She shook her hand, dropping the charred remains of the folder to the floor, and sucked her finger. Catie looked down, and was dismayed to see ash everywhere.

Well, what did you expect? Who daydreams about a guy while holding something that is actually on fire?

"Shit," she said aloud.

She stamped out the little bits that still glowed with the toe of her high heel, feeling the draft from the window on her bare legs. January was not the ideal time to leave a window open in New York, especially not when you were wearing your favorite white flowy dress. It was out of season, but there was space to hide her little memo pad, and her boobs looked killer in it. And, well, maybe she did want to attract Jake, even if she wouldn't know what to do if it happened.

Catie dropped to her knees and started desperately collecting the bits of paper that hadn't burned all the way while trying to brush the rest of the ash into the carpet. She couldn't imagine what she'd say if someone came in right now. She didn't think there was any way this situation could get more vulnerable.

Until she felt a huge gust of air and her dress flew up and over her back, revealing her little white thong to whoever was behind her. Because someone was behind her — they'd opened the door, pulling in that gust of wind. Catie bit her lip and looked over her shoulder.

Jake, the mystery Dom, stood over her, his dark eyes burning and his face unreadable. He didn't speak, but she could feel his eyes raking across her body. His broad chest rose slowly with one deep breath, and his jaw clenched. Just the sight of him stunned her into silence. She was never at a loss for words — *never* — but somehow, the words wouldn't form. Her limbs wouldn't move. She was paralyzed, frozen in an in between state; she didn't know if she were humiliated, afraid, or turned on.

When her brain started working again, she thought: *Why hasn't he said anything?*

But Jake had come into the room, and was already closing the door behind him.

chapter 2

Jake Jayson worked very hard not to have an inappropriate reaction to the scene that greeted him when he opened Lola's door. What he wanted to do first was laugh out loud. The last thing he'd expected to see when he came into Lola's office was Catie Roberts on her hands and knees with her skirt flying up around her head like some crazy combination of Marilyn Monroe and Lucille Ball.

What he wanted to do after that would have made Catie blush if she'd known about it. In more than one place.

But none of that was material. He had to be on his guard around Catie, given his attraction to her. 'Attraction' seemed like such an inadequate word. The time she spent in the lounge while he indulged his hobby—fine, call it nostalgia—of tending bar these past few months had been, in its own way, torturous. He was forever, constantly aware of where she was. She pulled at him in a way he could never quite define, like she carried a powerful charge opposite his own. Under different circumstances, he would have delved into that attraction; he would have delved into *her*, relishing each and every last bit of discovery. But as it was, she was a novice. She had no real experience, at least none that he was aware of, and she had not been trained. And novices often had a tendency to become attached to their trainers. It was one reason he didn't train. It would be manifestly unfair to the girl to give in to his desires, knowing he could never offer her more than domination and sex.

And, perhaps more importantly, there was always something else about her, something he would catch in stray moments when she thought no one was watching. Something he couldn't identify, couldn't name, but that made her seem vulnerable underneath her often glib exterior. Something that made him sure he would only hurt her more if he had her the way he wanted, and then, as always, proved himself incapable of a normal human relationship.

So he had done his best to stay away. Not that that did him any good now, with her ass in the air in front of him.

Even so, he was grateful to her for making him feel good, as she so often did without knowing it. Especially now that he'd just come from another board meeting at Stephan's House. Now was a very good time for something to come along and help him feel good.

Which was why he was so dismayed when he took in the rest of the scene and pieced together what she'd been doing. Or at least the bare outlines of it. Why she'd want to burn a manila folder in the middle of Lola's office was still a mystery.

"What were you doing?" he said quietly.

Catie leaned back on her calves, her fingers leaving dull streaks of ash on her pretty white dress, and looked up at him with huge blue eyes. She looked sad, defeated. Disappointed. In herself? And yet relieved.

That she stayed on her knees in his presence only tormented him. The image of Catie looking at up at him with those red lips wrapped around his cock flashed unbidden in his mind.

"I asked you a question," he said.

"Oh God," she said, wringing her hands. "Please don't tell."

She wiped her face with the back of her hand, and Jake realized she'd started to cry. He felt a surge of something, something unfamiliar: he wanted to protect her.

From what? She has obviously done something.

"Tell me," he said, striding toward her, half wishing she would get up so he could stop thinking about her natural submissiveness. "Now."

"I was…" She looked about, at all the evidence strewn around the ground, at the still recognizable chunk of manila folder where she'd dropped it. It was clear she was casting about for a story.

"Don't lie to me, Catie," he said.

"If I tell you the truth, I lose everything," she said, so softly he wasn't sure he was supposed to hear it.

She looked up at him with those sad eyes again, and he clenched his fists to keep from touching her. In another moment, he might have. Except for the sound of footsteps in the hall.

Catie hissed as she sucked in her breath, and Jake's own shoulders stiffened. This was not the kind of moment that benefitted from interruption. His mind was already going through everything he knew, objectively, about Catie Roberts, everything he could call upon that had nothing to do with his physical reaction to her: she had not chosen a trainer, even after several months. She made Lola nervous. No one knew much about her, except presumably Roman, who had approved her application. This was someone who had something to hide, or believed she did, and was obviously living in fear.

She might never tell anyone if no one stood up for her.

"If anyone comes in, I will tell them that this is part of a scene," he said. "You do not have to be afraid."

Most of the fear left her eyes, to be slowly replaced with…something else. She flushed.

He realized, *I called it a scene. I made her think…*

"Catie, you must tell me," he said, aware now of the full danger of this interaction. It wasn't just his attraction he had to guard against. It was hers.

She bit her lip, as though coming to a decision, and put her hand down on the carpet to steady herself as she got up from the floor. That was a relief to him, at least. Perhaps he could think straight if she weren't kneeling in front of him.

But as she bent over, a small memo pad fell from

the little hollow between her breasts, a natural pocket created by the cut of the dress. Jake watched it almost in slow motion, as though some part of his brain knew immediately what it must be for. There was a pause during which neither of them moved or spoke. They both just stared at the memo pad. Maybe he was imagining it. Nothing about this felt ordinary any longer.

"Give it to me," he finally said.

Refusing to look at him, she picked up the memo pad and rose, handing it to him. Then she simply stood there, frozen in place.

He flipped through the pages. They were notes in some sort of personalized shorthand, but he recognized enough to confirm what he feared. There was "ML" — Mistress Lola. And "MR," for Master Roman.

And there, on so many pages, was "Jake."

"Catie," he said, his voice dangerously calm, "explain."

~ ~ ~

Catie could barely think, there were so many different feelings shooting around inside her. She was afraid, of course. She was terrified. Jake was holding her book. He was *looking* at her book. Even if he couldn't decipher her notes, he'd know she was a liar.

She should be dealing with that. She should be dealing with that awful calamity, that utter catastrophe that was about to ruin everything. But her body was so buzzed by his presence, by the tone of his voice, by the way he'd ordered her around…

Oh God, think, Catie, think!

She could smell him. He smelled like sweat and spice. Her whole body tingled when he spoke.

"Catie, please do not make me ask you again."

She forced herself to look up at him. His eyes had darkened, and his expression had become grim. This was bad. His anger was frightening in a way, like a slow, cold cloud rolling in over the flat sky. Not in a violent way, but in a way that felt terrible to her: he'd think less of her. It only made her want him more.

What is wrong with me?

"Ok," she said, taking a breath. She could do this. She was an actress, for Pete's sake. "It's for my thesis. School."

She'd always had a fantasy of being a respected classicist somewhere, flying around giving lectures on the stuff she used to read about when she was little. She'd found the books in her dad's office and read, at first because she thought her dad was interested in Marcus Aurelius and the ancient Greeks and the rest. By the time she figured out the books were just for show, she really was into all of it. She used to pretend she was a great scholar. The memory was a happy one, until she remembered that Jake actually was supposed to be an academic. An adjunct professor? Guest lecturer? Something at one of the big New York schools. In what? Crap, that was important…

"Your thesis," he said. His eyes bore into her, pinning her in place.

"I know, it's not…ok, it's not as bad as it looks, I promise," she said, warming to her subject.

"Chivalry and BDSM and gender roles. I know that doesn't sound all that impressive to you—"

"Tell me where you are enrolled."

He really didn't ask questions so much as state the prerequisite to whatever he wanted you to say next.

"It's a working title," she trailed off. Jake's expression was unyielding. Didn't he believe her? It was a lie, but it was a good one. If he was at one of the famous schools, she'd better name one of the others. "City community college. Part time."

He looked down at the notepad again, flipping through some more pages. Every new page seemed to enflame him further, every new page another example of her deceit. She felt worse with every flip.

"Is this why you've never chosen a trainer?" he asked. "Why you've never ventured into any classes—never participated in a scene? I've noticed you, Catie, hanging back and watching. Observing."

She didn't answer immediately. How could she? He took another step toward her, and she flinched. His expression softened.

"I don't hurt people, Catie," he said. "Not unless they ask me to."

He stood so close to her that she could feel his breath on her cheek, could see the gentle rise of his chest underneath his Oxford shirt. He was in street clothes, a sort of professor-casual look, with a well-tailored grey blazer over his white button-down shirt and dark slacks. Where had he come from?

You're getting hysterical, Catie. Concentrate.

Yes, she had to concentrate. Had to think her

way out of this predicament. And yet, all she could focus on was the hollow at the base of his neck, the little dip in his collarbone, with a few curls of hair peeking up from his unbuttoned collar.

She reached out to touch it.

Lightning quick, he grabbed her wrist. His fingers burned into her. She nearly wilted from that touch, and looked up only when she heard him grunt.

For a long moment, they stood there like that, neither of them moving.

When Jake spoke, his voice was rough. "Quickly, Catie, tell me: are you only here to observe all the freaks? Is that your only reason for being at Club Volare?"

"No." She was surprised to find she meant it.

"Then why haven't you chosen a trainer? Why haven't you committed?"

"I only wanted you, and you won't look at me," she blurted out.

Immediately she wished there was somewhere to hide, but Jake didn't release her, and she didn't think she could have moved even if he had. What she'd said had been absolutely true, and she knew that he knew it. It was humiliating, and exposing, and pathetic, and thrilling to know she had just put herself in his power. His expression had frozen, a flat, unreadable mask, except for the pulsing of a vein in his forehead. His grip on her wrist tightened imperceptibly.

Oh God, what had she done?

"I don't... I didn't mean... This is just how I try to understand things—by studying them, by watching. I've just been too scared to jump in. I'm not the cannonballing type. And I was never going to out anyone, I promise, it was just…academic."

How many lies can you tell at once, Catie? At least one of those things had been true.

She hated herself, but it's not like she could tell the truth. Telling the truth would mean she'd lose her shot to save what was left of her family. And it would mean that this man she craved in some incomprehensible way would walk away from her forever.

He might do that anyway. She might lose everything anyway. It was all up to him.

"What if you trained me?" she said suddenly.

Jake had been frozen in some sort of controlled Zen state, but this jolted him out of it.

"Catie…" he said.

She didn't want to hear all the reasons he couldn't do it. It was her only shot, and the thing she truly wanted. She'd figure out how it was going to work with all her lies and planned betrayal later.

"You can train me," she went on, "and you can read all my notes. You can read the paper before I hand it in. I'll obey you in everything, take out whatever you want me to take out. Please," she begged. "*Please* just don't tell anyone."

Jake inhaled deeply. He looked like Dr. Jekyll on the verge of turning into Mr. Hyde. Catie was ashamed to find that she wanted them both. She opened her mouth to speak, but he put his fingers to his lips, silencing her.

"Do not speak over me again, Catie, not in this context. That is the first thing you will learn, and you will learn it right now."

She nodded slowly, afraid to break his gaze. Did this mean…

"Ethically, I must consult with Master Roman. I will promise not to reveal your secret, as far as those ethics allow. But that does not mean you will be allowed to stay, or that I will agree to train you."

For all his calm, formal language, Jake was breathing hard. He hadn't let go of her wrist.

"I understand," she said, looking at the floor.

"No, you do not. I am going to speak with Roman now. You will wait here for me." She felt his thumb move against the inside of her wrist and suppressed a shiver. He continued, "Naked."

It took her a moment to comprehend. *Wait— naked?*

She said, "This is Lola's office…"

Jake squeezed her wrist before letting it drop to her side. Her skin felt cold where he no longer touched her, and she looked up at him imploringly.

"Naked," he repeated. "Strip."

He stepped back from her, as though to get a good view. *This is what it's about*, she thought, feeling slightly dizzy. *This is how it works.* A rush of adrenaline flooded her system, covering the guilt she still felt for lying, and spiking physical sensation in her entire body. She became aware of the heat growing in her pelvis, of the dull, thudding, drive building there. Her nipples grew tight in demanding little points under her thin dress, evidence of her desire.

He'll see that…

"Right now, Catie."

The window behind her was still open to the cold January air, but she could barely feel it for the heat rushing through her body. She locked eyes with Jake as she shrugged off one shoulder strap, then the other. He didn't look away, didn't reprimand her for what felt like a challenge. Catie wasn't exactly sure what was happening. She wanted to obey, but she also wanted to fight him, and then she wanted him to win. So she locked eyes with him the whole time, until she stood before him completely naked.

After a moment, he gave the barest hint of a smile.

"You will wait here until I release you," he said.

And then he was gone.

chapter 3

Jake barely escaped with his mind still intact. He had never wanted a woman so badly in his entire life. The way she looked at him! She was a sub who issued challenges without even knowing it. Did she know what kind of dance that was? Impossible. The way she'd looked at him....

It had only been a few minutes. His world had been upended in only a few minutes.

He stalked through the dimly lit halls of Volare NY, arguing with himself. Neither the Zen simplicity of the lines nor the rich sensuality of the fabrics did anything to calm him. He knew people were watching. He was famous for his reserve, his stern fortitude, his severity, and now he paced the halls muttering to himself. Well, let them watch.

Let her wait.

Oh God.

The thought of her—the memory of her— waiting for him, naked... He stopped abruptly. Why had he done that? He'd already engaged in a scene with her, without thinking, without negotiation, on the pretense of further thought. He never acted so impulsively. He was never *moved* to act so impulsively.

And he *must* think about it. Away from her. Away from the deafening lust she aroused in him. He'd wanted her since the moment he'd first seen her, but he had dealt with that with avoidance, and it had been manageable, if only barely. But somehow it was worse now, following this discovery. This...violation. There'd been something in her eyes, something beneath all the fear and sadness and regret—she *liked* getting caught. Did she really?

He felt his abdominals coil inside him and he licked his lips. It was impossible that he could make a rational decision in the grips of this...whatever it was. Lust. It was lust.

But hadn't he always wanted to feel this strongly, about anything? It wasn't love, but it was passion, of a kind. He *wanted*. He *felt*.

That might make him a terrible trainer. But she'd said he was the only one she'd wanted. Dare he believe her?

No, that part had been true. There had been more lies in the things she'd said, maybe more even than she'd intended. And he would discover them all. But that part had been true.

"Damn!"

He'd come to Roman's office. The heavy, dark

wooden door cracked slightly open, indicating Roman's availability. Roman was not just the Master of Volare NY; he was Jake's friend. He had saved Jake's life, as far as Jake was concerned, when he'd brought him into Volare. Roman would offer him good counsel.

So why did he hesitate?

Slow down. Think.

He had promised not to reveal her betrayal. Why had he done that? That had been unnecessary and unwise. He hadn't thought; he'd just done it. Again, unlike him. And yet now that the promise was made, he couldn't break it. That was a line he simply refused to cross.

And there was another promise he was bound to keep. A promise that said he couldn't turn away from someone in need of help. Someone who was lost. That was the look he'd first seen when he'd caught her: she'd been lost, and afraid, and alone.

That was it. Her lies, her challenge—strength covering weakness, an offense hiding a wound. That was something with which he was familiar, that was something his heart—what there was of it—recognized immediately, even if it took his mind a moment to catch up. Perhaps that was what had drawn him to her all along.

Yet, it also left him with only two options. He could accept her as a trainee, take the duty seriously, try to ignore his own passions and hope to bring her far enough along that she would no longer consider the publication of anything that might be harmful to Volare. After all, she already had the information. She'd already been here...how long? Months? Long enough to do some damage if she felt like it.

And his second option was what? To kick her out. No. He already knew he wouldn't do that. He'd already committed himself to that, hadn't he?

He had. The minute he'd promised not to reveal what she'd done. The minute he'd ordered her to strip. He'd already made his decision without thinking it through, without considering all the angles, and without consulting with Roman, as he was obligated to do.

What had come over him?

Hadn't he always wanted this? Something that made him feel enough to compel him to...do anything? Something? Even if it was only lust, it was...

Human.

So why did he feel nearly nauseous?

"When the gods wish to punish us, they answer our prayers," he said to himself, and opened Roman's door.

Roman sat at his desk, his distinguished jaw resting in his hand as he surveyed Lola with a look of amused boredom. Jake knew it was the sort of thing that would infuriate Lola, and knew that it in fact had infuriated her, based on how rigid she held her back as she went through the binder that she held on her lap. Neither of them would ever admit to provoking the other, of course.

And there, between them, knelt a naked woman with a ball gag in her mouth.

Jake cleared his throat.

"Jacob." Lola gave him a warm smile, perhaps warmer than she might have if she was not in the middle of sparring — on some level — with Roman.

She'd always told Jake that he reminded her of her brother, and by some small stroke of luck, Jake had never found himself attracted to the voluptuous redhead. They were genuine friends.

So he knew she'd forgive his rudeness.

"What do you know of Catie?" he said abruptly. The hoarseness of his own voice surprised him. He sounded like he'd just run a marathon overnight to get this particular intelligence about Catie.

He felt that desperate, too.

Roman smiled that slow, cat-like smile, but otherwise didn't move a muscle. "I approved her application personally," he said.

"That's not what I asked."

"But that's the answer you have been given."

There was a tense silence, and then Lola laughed. She said, "Just do what you have to do, please. I have a lot to do today, and Roman's attention is difficult enough to commandeer without this silverback posturing."

"Party planning is boring," Roman sighed.

"It is not a party," Lola said. "It is the Valentine's Auction—our major yearly event, and our biggest fundraiser, and we have to do it all in secret. It is *not* a party; it is an event. Speaking of which..." Her laser focus shifted to Jake, and he suddenly realized he'd interrupted Lola while she was in the middle of Organizing, which was a little like walking into a tornado. But her eyes softened as she said, "This year, I thought the proceeds would benefit Stephan's House. I know you're planning an expansion, and I thought Volare could help. With your ok, of course."

Jake was bewildered. He felt as though his head

had been removed, placed in a paint-shaker, and then screwed back on the wrong way. He'd come here to talk about *Catie*. Not his brother. Not his charity.

"Yes, of course," he said. "But about Catie…"

Lola's green eyes narrowed. "Yes, I'd like to hear about Catie, too."

Roman stretched his back and neck with that peculiar refined animalism that was so characteristic of him, and rose to his full six-foot height. "There is nothing more to say," he said.

Jake frowned. "That's not quite true. I learned something about her that might pose a threat to Volare."

The silence that followed was like a vacuum, needing to be filled. There were two dimples in Lola's forehead, the ones that formed when she became worried.

Jake took a deep breath. He'd have to disclose his stupidity one way or the other. "I promised not to reveal it. I think I can contain the situation if I act as Catie's trainer, but I am…concerned…about my ability to do so. Objectively. Without a conflict of interest."

Lola and Roman spoke at the same time.

"She's asked you to be her trainer?"

"What conflict of interest? Because of your interest in her?"

The Master and Mistress of Volare NY looked at each other and smiled. Sometimes it seemed as though they could read each other's minds. Jake often wondered if they'd be happier together, but no one — *no one* — ever broached that particular topic.

"Yes to both of you," Jake answered. He didn't like the glint in Roman's eye, didn't like the suggestion that Roman knew quite a bit more than he was saying. But he also knew how these things went. Roman had his code, just like Jake. And his own reasons for honoring it.

Now Roman let himself look truly happy and reached down to stroke the back of the gagged woman's head. Lola turned away slightly.

"I trust you," Roman said. "Whatever you decide, Jacob. I would be happy to see Catie participate. There is…"

"Something about her," Jake finished. His heart was thudding against his ribcage. The sight of the naked, gagged woman reminded him of how he'd left Catie. The idea of anyone else walking in on her made his blood pound painfully in his head. The knowledge that she waited like that in obedience to *him* made it throb in an altogether different way.

Roman looked at him carefully. "Be careful, old friend."

"Yes."

"But not too careful."

And then Roman smiled, his white teeth flashing. If Jake had the resources to devote to solving puzzles, he would have interrogated his old friend, would have tried to figure out what pleased Roman so much about this, what the man saw that Jake didn't. But there was simply not enough blood left in his brain for such an endeavor.

No. You must control yourself. This proposition— this idea that he would train Catie, that he would oversee her work for the sake of Volare—it was only palatable if he could tell himself he was helping her, too. Helping whatever part of her was lost and wounded, whatever it was he had seen in those blue eyes. Without that focus, he might simply lose himself in lust.

Like a man made of metal and restraint, he pivoted his head to look at Lola. "Mistress Lola, might I beg a favor?"

She smiled at his formality. "Yeah, I suppose."

"Stay away from your office for a short while."

~ ~ ~

Catie had begun to shiver. Her body was covered in gooseflesh, and her nipples were almost painfully hard. Her mind had been racing since Jake had left her—naked, alone—in Lola's office. Her thoughts had begun to spin so fast that they'd lost all sense of proportion and balance, and she'd found herself thinking crazy things: *He's told everyone. They're all watching. They all hate you. They will punish you.*

And yet she was wet. She could feel the cold January air on the wetness still seeping between her legs. The thought of being punished by Jake was...

"Oh God, what is wrong with me?" she said aloud.

The sound of her own voice startled her. The following silence seemed to heighten her solitude, like a persistent ringing in her ears that just kept getting worse. Anyone could come in at any time. She should leave. She was probably about to be exposed, she was about to lose everything, and the only thing she couldn't handle would be...to be cast out. To be totally rejected by these people—and this place—that she'd come to like. She wanted to be at home here. Wanted to be a part of it. She genuinely loved the ethos: to know yourself and to help others.

No, she couldn't handle it if they kicked her out. If she had to face them, knowing they knew her for what she was and hated her... She didn't know why, exactly, but the thought sent her into a panic, and she shied away from it. She should leave. She should run away before...

But then she'd remind herself that she believed Jake, for some reason. Believed his promises. It made her realize how much she normally disbelieved: no one ever really did what they said they would. No one could really be relied upon.

But she didn't have any reason to believe him more than she believed anyone else, beyond how she'd felt when he'd looked at her. She really was being a fool.

This back and forth went on and on, the volume steadily rising with each volley, each thought building upon the last, until she thought she would actually lose her mind.

And then, the door opened.

Jake stood there, towering over her with his dark eyes and his dark hair that had come slightly unkempt. He looked like authority personified. He walked in and quickly closed the door behind him, and his eyes never left her body as he did so. Catie felt herself blush. With apparent effort, he lifted his gaze and looked her in the eye.

"Kneel," he said.

Catie startled, suddenly pulling out of her

crazed thoughts and back to the present. She wasn't sure if she'd heard him correctly. "What?"

"*Kneel.*"

She felt nervous, and instinctively tried to grab at the fabric of her dress, an old habit that gave her something to do with her hands when she felt uneasy, but this only reminded her that she wasn't wearing a dress. She was naked. She blushed all over again, and then she saw the look in Jake's eyes, and felt again that unfamiliar mix of fear and arousal.

She fumbled slightly getting to her knees. When she did, she sat back on her calves, as she had before, and looked up at him.

Just looking up at him gave her a little twitch down below. She heard his intake of breath and grew worried.

"Did I do something wrong?" she asked.

"No," he said. His voice sounded hoarse. "A good beginning."

She suppressed a smile. Why did that feel so good? It was like a different flavor of good from when she'd provoked his disapproval and the implied threat of discipline, but still sweet. Sweet, as opposed to spicy.

"Catie, pay attention," he said, and she focused on him. He was perfectly still. Almost unnaturally still. She hadn't realized how much normal people moved when they weren't thinking about it until confronted with this absolute, controlled stillness.

"If I am to train you, we must first negotiate the nature and method of your training."

"Ok," she said. "That makes sense."

His chest expanded as he took a great breath.

The moment stretched while Catie wondered what she'd done wrong.

He said, "You will address me as 'sir' while in session."

She blinked. Of course. "Yes, sir."

"Are you cold?"

Catie had almost begun to feel normal in her nudity, even sitting — kneeling — before a fully clothed man. As though it were just an everyday thing. Now she remembered her nakedness and felt a renewed gush of pleasure at the thought. She looked down at her nipples; they were still hard. And she didn't feel cold. Well, she did, but not unpleasantly so. It added something.

"I don't think so," she said carefully.

"Be precise. You must always be precise about what you feel, or things might go very badly."

"I am, but I don't want you to close the window," she said. And then a little shamefacedly, "I think I like it."

He gave the briefest of smiles. "Good."

Catie preened.

Jake began to walk around her in a circle, looking her up and down. She turned her head to follow him, but snapped her head forward again at the merest look from him. For some reason his expression was easy to read — easier than others' — and she was good with most people. Acting had taught her to look for and respond to emotion. But with Jake, it was almost like she didn't have a choice.

"You are aware of what Volare is about?" he said.

"Yes." There was a pause. She added, "Sir."

"Then tell me."

Catie hadn't expected to be grilled. It felt like a school examination, and she was gripped with the anxiety of being terminally unprepared, even though she knew this. Didn't she? She racked her brain.

"It's about knowing yourself by testing your limits. Knowing yourself so well that you can be of use. And service." She tried desperately to remember the motto. Something about flying? Learning to fly through the practice? "About helping?"

"Close enough." She thought she heard him smile. "Yes, knowing yourself through exploration of the extremes, of one's boundaries. And then some people use that knowledge to ultimately be of service to others, though it's not required. And then throughout it all is the incredible sex."

"Oh thank God," she said, and then immediately clamped her hand over her mouth. A second later, she removed it. "*Sir*," she added.

She heard a chuckle, and then his hand was on her shoulder. It was large, larger than she'd expected, but smooth. And warm. So very, very warm. He kept it there while he moved around her, until he stood very close to her face. She couldn't help but notice she was just about at the perfect height for…

"Catie," he said.

Would she do it? If he asked her to suck him off, right here? If he *ordered* her to? The truth was, she wanted to. She couldn't help but wonder what he looked like, how big he was, what he'd taste like…

"Look up," he said.

She did. He looked down at her, and she could see the desire in his face. He threaded his fingers through the hair at the back of her head and she bit her lip.

"You are up to date with the club-mandated tests?"

He meant STD tests. She nodded. "Of course."

"So am I."

She thought about what that meant and shivered.

Jake said, "Do you understand what this means? It means I will fuck you. You will be mine for the duration of training, and that means you are asking a great deal of me. I will do my best, but I demand total honesty and total obedience, and I *will* punish you if you stray or if you lie to me. I will explore every last inch of you, Catie, inside and out, and you will hide nothing. Do you understand and agree?"

It was exactly what she couldn't do, what she couldn't agree to. And yet, Catie had never wanted anything more in her life. So she told one more lie.

"Yes, sir," she said.

His fingers tightened, pulling her head back slightly. She stifled a groan.

"Trainees sometimes become...attached," he said, and his voice had become a whisper. "That would be unwise. I do not become attached. It is not how I am built. Do not make the mistake of thinking that I am. As soon as our training commences, you must understand that it is both deeply personal and deeply impersonal at the same time. Individual feelings do not—"

"Has it commenced yet, sir?" she asked, looking

up into his eyes. Immediately, she realized that she'd interrupted him. Oh God, how she wanted him. *Him.* She wanted to make him come just once with her, Catie, not the trainee. And she wanted to know that he wanted her.

He didn't say anything. His jaw clenched and his fingers tightened their grip on her hair.

This is it, Catie.

She'd never know what gave her the courage, but in that moment, she reached for the zipper on his expensive slacks. She never got close enough to touch it. With a growl, he yanked her to her feet, dragged her over to the desk, and pushed her down on top of it. The look on his face was pure animal need, and it was exactly what she wanted to see. She didn't know where it had come from or who she had become, suddenly, without warning, but she knew what she wanted. She wanted him to take her, hard.

Jake held her there while he freed his cock, his eyes locked on hers. He pushed himself between her legs and paused for just a second, still holding her down. His eyes flashed and something churned deep within him.

"Please," she said. "Quickly."

He snarled, and then he plunged into her and fell on her neck, biting her and stretching her to her limit all at once. It hurt, and she loved the pain and the feeling of fullness together, complementing each other. She'd thought about this so many times, so many ways...

He fucked her hard, pounding deep into her again and again, and it sent her over the edge almost too quickly. She felt her inner muscles contract in quick spasms before the rest of her was ready and primed, and she was building for her second before she even knew what happened. Jake lifted her legs and hips off of the desk to go deeper, and when he drove into her this time, he looked her right in the eye and let her know he owned her.

She came again, and again, and again.

chapter 4

It had been a long week since Jake had discovered Catie in Lola's office. A week since he'd agreed to train her, a week since his first—second?—incredible error of judgment regarding that woman. His mind kept returning to it in the least helpful of ways, reminding him that he should have been thinking about what he'd learned, how to design her training. Instead, he thought about what she'd felt like inside, like warm, wet velvet, and he'd thought about the look in her eyes, like she wanted to both fight and fuck, and the way she'd wanted it hard, just like he wanted to take her. He thought about the way she'd looked embarrassed when she'd said she wanted only him. He thought about that a lot.

No matter what his responsibilities, no matter

how inappropriate the time or place, if he left his mind unoccupied for a moment, there she was.

And there was no more inappropriate time or place than right now or right here. He sat in the small office he kept at the back of the top floor of the haven he'd built for addicts, runaways, those in danger of hurting themselves. Stephan's House. And he was waiting for Eileen Corrigan, Stephan's mother.

He rearranged the many papers on his desk, all the things having to do with the new expansion, and leaned his head back against the old exposed brick. This building would be worth eight figures if he ever decided to sell it. He wouldn't. The location, in the East Village, was too convenient for kids who might suddenly decide to get help. You never wanted to miss a walk-in.

What could she possibly want?

He hadn't seen Eileen Corrigan in five years. He didn't like to think about how she'd looked at him then. He would probably remember it for the rest of his life. There hadn't been any tears. Just pure, unadulterated hatred.

He didn't like to think about how she'd ever looked at him, if he were being honest, but when he was younger he could pretend, in the way boys do. And there was always Stephan and his father, and together they'd always gone off somewhere, away from Eileen Corrigan's angry banging of pots and pans and muttered comments. In retrospect, it was likely that this was no accident.

His father had always had a talent for social situations. Jake had at least tried to learn to mimic that skill, if not embody it, the way his father and

Stephan had.

"Sleeping on the job, huh?"

He snapped his head up and opened his eyes. There she was, Eileen Corrigan, in the flesh. She looked much older than he remembered, and yet somehow healthier. Her red hair was no longer permed, but was instead cropped in a modest bob. It struck him as matronly. Responsible, even. He felt disoriented; the Eileen Corrigan he had known had worn push-up bras to her son's parent-teacher conferences.

"Eileen."

"Don't get up, Jake." She sat down with alarming comfort on the chair opposite his desk. "We've got too much history for that crap."

"All right." He sat back down and looked at her. She met his gaze. She would. He suddenly realized he had no idea how to conduct this interview, and he was so unaccustomed to simply not knowing that he was now at a loss for words. He felt like almost anything he might say could be a horrible misstep, the kind of thing that would rend Eileen's wound in two. Or his own.

"Well, aren't you curious?" she said. She was almost smiling. Almost.

"Yes," he admitted. "Quite."

"The anniversary is coming up."

"I know."

"I see that you know. You're preparing all kinds of stuff, it looks like." She peered at the papers on his desk. "You've got quite a good operation going on here. I'm impressed."

He winced, and she noticed it.

"I meant that, Jacob," she said, and opened her

purse, which he noticed was now a sedate cream color, rather than the lime green he remembered. "You done good."

When he was sure he could speak normally, he said, "Thank you."

Eileen lit a cigarette, ignoring the 'no smoking' sign, and Jake was almost relieved to see some things hadn't changed. Maybe that was why he suddenly felt like himself again.

"Eileen, what do you want?"

Now she did smile.

"I want to help out," she said. "I want to work here. Get involved."

"No." The word was out before he could even think it. More followed. "I'm sorry, but I can't—"

"I have a right," she said quietly.

He couldn't argue with that. He couldn't even put forth an argument as to why he didn't want her there, besides the fact that it would be a constant reminder that he should feel terrible for the rest of his life. Here, in this place, in his attempt to...

No, he'd never make it right. He knew that; making it right wasn't the point. The point was to be better and hope it was good enough. And Eileen's presence might make that harder.

"Can't there be somewhere else?" he said. "Why here? Why does it have to be here?"

She didn't answer. Just stared at him. It had been a terrible thing to say.

"I'm sorry," he said, and watched his hand flex uselessly on the surface of his desk, trying desperately to work off the nervous tension. He couldn't bring himself to look at her after he'd said that. To his surprise he saw her hand come into his view, almost in slow motion. It came to a rest atop his own, and gently squeezed.

"I don't hate you, Jakey," she said.

He was suddenly repelled. It was a familiar feeling, that repulsion to a gesture of affection and intimacy, and then there was another wave of it, close on the crest of the first, at his own reaction to another human being's attempt to show him kindness, or closeness, or whatever it was normal people had when they reached across a table in a moment of remembered pain to squeeze someone else's hand.

He pulled his hand away, hating himself and his heartlessness afresh. "I'm sorry, Eileen," he said, still unable to look at her. Instead, he stared resolutely at a bronze paperweight, some award he'd been given for civic service. The irony burned. "Of course you're right. I'll speak with Lina and explain. She'll put you wherever you're needed."

Another plume of smoke was propelled into his field of vision, and he knew she was studying him. It added another level of...something...to his already considerable discomfort. He felt she truly *saw*, because she knew. She was the only person left alive who really knew.

"Ok, Jake," she finally said. "I'll talk to Lina."

With relief, he let his shoulders relax and watched her back as she walked to the door. She turned and watched him for a moment, her expression sad. Then she said, "See you around," and closed the door behind her.

After Eileen left, Jake had been fairly useless.

He'd tried, for a few hours, to do only the things he could do — calls to licensing boards, politicians, the sort of networking stuff he was uniquely positioned for given his family ties — but it was soon late on a Friday afternoon, and he knew his peers would all be well on their way to their weekend homes. All that was left was what he thought of as actual work, and he simply could not concentrate. After he'd lost the thread in yet another planning conversation, Lina had sent him home.

"That's an order, boss," she'd said firmly.

And so once again, his mind was left unoccupied, and once again thoughts of Catie rushed in to fill the vacuum. Only now, the general atmosphere was tainted with the experience of Eileen Corrigan's visit and all the tired, awful memories that it dredged up.

He thought he'd walk home, which, in retrospect, was ridiculous; it was a long way to his townhouse in the East Fifties. And it did nothing to clear his mind. He finally caught a cab — difficult to do with the light, warm rain, which was unseasonable for January — and brooded until he arrived at his door.

He lived alone. Most men in his position had an assistant or a secretary or something, or what in another age might have been called a 'valet' or a 'manservant' or even a 'butler,' but Jake had never felt comfortable with personal servants. The idea of another person who would be cognizant of every little thing in his life felt unnatural, suffocating. He knew most people wouldn't have felt that way, but he supposed that the closeness of others was something you had to get used to very young or not at all.

As soon as he'd punched in the security code, he removed his coat and headed straight for the library. It was the only room he hadn't had redecorated since he'd inherited the house after his mother's death, and it was the only room his mother had had no use for. It was where Jake had always kept his things.

In particular, it housed the projector and the collection of movies he'd been given, so far back in the hazy reaches of his memory that he could never be sure which distant relative was responsible for the gift. It might have just as easily been a generous friend of his mother's, though he couldn't imagine any of that crowd with a particular taste for old Hollywood. Well, perhaps some of the more stylish men. Maybe someone just wanted to share their love of Sunset Boulevard with him.

Well, whoever it was, he was grateful now. He'd been grateful then. There was never anything quite so soothing as losing yourself in those perfectly constructed worlds, no matter what else was going on around you. His first lessons in how to be a man had come from Humphrey Bogart and Cary Grant.

But now he didn't need to be reminded of what it was to be man. He felt that altogether too deeply. Right now, he needed to forget as much as possible, as quickly as possible. Something that fit his mood, that wouldn't remind him of all the normal, human things he'd proved himself incapable of over the years. Not a romance, then. Not a comedy where everyone ends up in love and happy. He crossed the dark room, navigating the antique furniture from memory, and turned on the standing lamp near his old reels. He'd had the reels updated in the past few years, though it was damned expensive to find some of them in actual film.

The Big Sleep. Perfect. Bogey and Bacall in the film version of Raymond Chandler's first noir novel, where nothing is as it seems and none of the endings are happy.

He set up the projector, mixed himself a drink, turned off the light, and sat back to forget.

He watched perhaps thirty seconds of the film before he realized his mistake. Lauren Bacall. She walked on screen and there was no point in looking at anyone else. She sparred and fought with Bogey's Philip Marlowe like she wanted to lose, and there was no help for it: he saw Catie in her.

Catie.

There was no getting away from her. It was his own fault, his own weakness, his own despicable, despicable weakness. He'd simply been overwhelmed. No, there was no "simply"; he was a Dom who'd ceded control of himself to lust. There was nothing more frightening. Nothing less forgivable. He should have been able to resist Catie's advances, because he knew better, knew the potential complications of personal entanglements between a trainer and a trainee, and worse, knew his own limitations. And he'd been completely helpless.

Yet wasn't that in and of itself remarkable? He'd been helpless, overcome by something he wanted. The only other time he was ever overcome was when he was seized by revulsion at some innocently gesture of affection, as he had been when Eileen Corrigan tried to hold his hand.

He was tired of trying to figure that particular puzzle out. He'd been to numerous psychiatrists, and in the end the best he could do was to say those intimacies felt like lies, and he recoiled. It never changed.

The projector continued to roll behind him, the soft *thwip thwip* of the film barely audible under the dialog. Bacall was dressing Bogey down, reading the poor man like a book from head to toe. Bogey looked like someone who'd been surprised with a cigar and a slap, and was smiling just from confusion.

Jake recognized the look.

There hadn't been sweet nothings with Catie on that desk, but when he'd looked at her, when she'd been underneath him...he could have sworn that she understood. What he'd wanted was exactly what she'd wanted, reflected from the other side. It wasn't looking back at it and observing that fact that disturbed him; it was that he had been absolutely sure of it at the time. There hadn't been an ambiguity, no doubt. Wasn't that more intimate than anything he'd ever experienced? And yet there'd been no revulsion.

Jake sipped his drink. No wonder he couldn't get her out of his mind. He was old enough that he didn't expect to experience many completely new things anymore, short of falling in love, which was impossible for him, or having children, which he thought would be irresponsible and even quite cruel, given his limitations.

Catie had been new.

This was problematic. His job as her trainer, and his obligation, was to explore *her*. To focus on her needs, her education. To help *her*. Not himself.

He struggled to think back on their brief interview without his desire getting in the way. He hadn't wanted someone so badly, so consistently, in his entire life, but damn it, he would do his job. He *would* help her. Because it was the only way he might begin to make up for losing control, for taking his own interest. And because, as she wavered into focus through his memory and his lust, what he saw was what he had first suspected: beneath it all, she was lost.

There were the lies, first and foremost. She was still lying, he was sure of it, but whether it was deliberate or instinctual, he didn't know. Jake was only half-watching the film. It was one he'd memorized, but its familiar storyline seeped into his thoughts: Bacall lies to protect her sister, her family, herself. Catie was protecting more than just her secret schoolwork. She was a natural sub, and possibly a masochist, and maybe many other delightful things he would eventually discover. She couldn't lie about any of that. He'd seen them, felt them. Volare should be a wonderland to her. And yet she'd sat on the sidelines for months, afraid to participate.

Why?

chapter 5

Five minutes before her first scheduled training session, Catie wanted to disappear. She wanted to turn back time, and...what?

What would she change to avoid where she'd ended up? Well, maybe she would have put a lo-jack ankle bracelet on her dad. If she could have prevented him from being, frankly, such a horrible person, maybe she wouldn't be in this position now. But she couldn't do any of that. She couldn't force her dad to be good, she couldn't force him to care, she couldn't force fate to give her back her family. So what was the point in wishing?

And now circumstances demanded that Catie be a horrible person, too.

She leaned back against the finely textured Volare wall, clinging to it for comfort, and surveyed the lounge. It was empty, thank God. Apparently Saturday mornings weren't a hugely popular time for the social areas of the club, though Catie could hear the occasional *thwap* coming from a private room somewhere nearby.

She didn't think she could handle having to keep up the charade in public right now. She had no idea how she was going to keep it up with Jake.

God. Jake.

Her belly fluttered, and her shaking hands gripped the wall behind her. Jake had wrecked her. She hadn't known it at the time; she hadn't known much of *anything* while he was inside her, on top of that desk. It really had felt like he'd been inside her head, like they'd known each other beyond words, and it had been…peaceful. Also violent and stormy and overwhelming, but at her core, she'd felt at home. He'd fucked her more thoroughly than any of the men she'd ever been with, mind *and* body.

She'd stumbled back to her friend Danny's apartment, where she was subletting his couch, shaken and unsure of what had just happened inside her. She'd tried telling herself that it was just sex. Just great sex. It didn't necessarily mean anything beyond well-matched pheromones and physical sensibilities. But as the week wore on, the memory of Jake's touch, of his voice, of his *control*, had worked its way through her mind like an invasive species. Everything she thought about— everything she tried to distract herself with— somehow led back to him. She'd chat with Danny about his auditions and callbacks and the gossip at the club where he worked as a bouncer, but Jake would be there, always, in the background. It didn't even make *sense*. It felt like she was losing her mind. Like she really was completely under his control, helpless to think about anything else.

And now she had to continue to lie to him.

She didn't know how she was going to do it. Obviously she'd lied to him the whole time she'd known him, but it was different now. It was like he'd discovered some part of her she hadn't even known existed, and yet she had deceived him about the most basic things. She didn't know if she *could* still do it.

Even if she did have a way out, even if she won the lottery—and she had bought an actual scratch ticket, in the kind of desperation you never want to tell anyone about, but she'd lost—she couldn't stop lying, could she? If she came clean, they would all hate her. She would *deserve* for them to all hate her. Jake would hate her.

Oh God, she thought, closing her eyes. *What am I going to do?*

Her phone buzzed madly inside her purse, like an answering call from the universe at large. Startled, she rummaged around until she found the thing, more to quiet her nerves than anything else.

It was a text from Brazzer.

Catie stopped breathing for a long, long moment. The intrusion of Brazzer into this place, into Volare itself, even if it was by text message…

Christ, what if someone had seen it?

She turned instinctively toward the wall, as if she needed the privacy, and feverishly mashed at the buttons of her phone.

More interest in this. Ur not only one on it.

I NEED A MEMBER LIST. Biographic
deets, shit they r into. Dont fuck up. Big $.

Catie's stomach flipped over. A member list. Biographical details. What people are into. Basically the worst privacy violation she could imagine, and someone else was "on it?"

Well, what did you expect?

Her dismay increased incrementally, like notes on a terribly discordant scale. She really hadn't thought this through. She'd only ever envisioned herself writing some sort of poetically philosophical think piece, with pseudonyms for all the members. Something literary. The kind of thing that communicated what Volare was really about, how it helped people, the sexy mystery of a secret society. Something classy. But then she'd taken it to freaking *Brazzer*, the guy who ran the worst tabloid in the country.

Because she knew he would pay.

And now there was someone else on it.

"Oh, Catie," she whispered to herself. "What have you done?"

With a sudden burst of energy, she looked around for the exit, as if reassuring herself that she could leave. She could run away. But even as she retraced the steps to the elevator that led back down to the normal world in her mind, she knew she couldn't bring herself to do it. She couldn't run away from these people, from Volare; they'd been *kind* to her, the closest thing she'd imagined to a family.

And, truthfully, she didn't think she was strong enough to run away from Jake. After just one time.

One time, and months of wondering about it. One perfect time.

She never would have guessed that being dragged up on a desk by her hair would feel "perfect," but that hadn't been the only surprise. It was insane, but as terrified as she was of being found out, when Jake was inside her, it had felt like he'd seen right through her. And he'd still wanted her.

Jake. Jake what? She didn't even know his last name. Didn't know the "biographical details," as Brazzer had put it. And Jake's warning—that he didn't grow attached, that he wasn't built that way—loomed in the background of her mind. So what that he wouldn't be attached—she couldn't allow herself to become attached, either. And she definitely couldn't afford to let him get close, or anywhere near the inside of her head, ever again. After all, she had no one else to rely on. It was all up to her.

"Oh, fuck me," she muttered.

"You can be sure of that."

Jake's voice slid across the room, smooth and slick, like spilled oil, and she could tell before she even saw him that he was be smiling. She saw him then, leaning against a far wall with his arms crossed, watching her from the shadows at the end of the bar. She was used to seeing him there at night, tending bar, chatting with people, holding court in his strange, guarded, gentlemanly way, watching over the whole club. She wasn't used to seeing him look back at her.

He looked good. Better than good. His physique was very noticeable under that finely cut suit, and the shadows accentuated the angles of his face. Catie began to feel her pulse throb in very unusual places.

"You're late," she said. He raised an eyebrow, and she realized her mistake. "No, you're not. I'm sorry."

The eyebrow stayed up.

"Sir," she added.

"You'll learn better than that," he said quietly.

The smile had faded from his face, replaced now by a look that might almost be concern. He pushed himself off the wall, and gestured towards the phone she still had in her hand.

"Bad news?" he asked.

Oh shit, he's been watching me. She racked her brain.

"I thought this wasn't supposed to get personal," she said, jutting her chin up at him. Was she reminding him, or trying to convince herself?

There was a pause, a moment of stillness. He studied her. Then he nodded, very slightly, and said, "Of course. Follow me."

Jake turned around and walked into the dark, winding halls of Volare.

chapter 6

Catie had to trot after him to catch up, her heels echoing off the dark hardwood floors. She followed him through the twisting halls and confusing layout, deep into the heart of the private rooms at Volare, where she'd never had reason to be before now. She found herself wondering why they'd chosen such a confusing layout, until they reached a room at the end of sudden turn, and then she guessed the reason: disorientation. They wanted you to feel like there was nothing else in the world besides the room you were in. Like there was nothing else happening besides what was happening to you.

The walk gave her time to think, which turned out to be both a blessing and a curse. That text message from Brazzer was still on her phone. She hadn't deleted it. What was she going to do? It seemed like she had only minutes to decide. She didn't want to have to figure all this out under Jake's intense stare.

Brazzer had said there was someone else on it. Would he have lied? Maybe it was just a way to spur her on. He'd been waiting for a long time. But now he seemed more sure that the story was real and would be a big draw. Someone else must have some information. Who? Would it be someone who knew anything? Who appreciated anything about Volare? Who cared about these people? What kind of story would they write if they didn't?

Catie bit her lip. That had sounded a lot like a rationalization. But it was a good rationalization, because it was true. Catie hadn't realized how important Volare had become to her. As strange as it might be, she had started to feel at home. She loved hanging out in the lounge at night when it was busy and had the feel of an intimate, old-timey social club where everyone knew each other, bonded by a common interest. She loved that everyone was expected to contribute to the charitable goals in some way, even if she still had no idea what the hell *she* was going to do. She loved that people naturally looked out for each other. She'd had about fifteen million offers of guidance, from mentoring to training to whatever, and none of them had felt skeezy. This place didn't deserve to be depicted as some kind of famous pervert's carnival sideshow playground.

And she was now the only one who could prevent that, even if it was her fault that the story would come to light in the first place.

She nearly bumped into Jake. They had come to the end of a particularly dark passage, and she could barely make out a large, ornate wooden door in front of him. Jake produced a key and opened the door.

It was pitch black inside the unknown room. Catie didn't move. She felt a hand wrap around her arm and pull her forward, past Jake's body, and then his hand was on the small of her back, pushing her into the blackness. She moved stiffly, stupidly afraid.

"Are you nervous?" he asked.

"Yes," she said. "And no."

"Do you trust me?"

Her heart beat against her chest, her breath felt shallow, the air felt thin, and his touch once again short-circuited something in her brain—and still, *still*, somewhere inside her, she was aware of the terrible, tragic irony: she did trust him. She just didn't deserve to.

"Yes, sir," she said. "I do."

She felt his hand brush her hair away from her neck, and then his lips moved against her ear. His touch spread a tingling wave over the surface of her skin, and the warmth of his body against hers gave her strength. She was already losing her mind to him.

"In this room, Catie, there are two requirements. They are not negotiable. They are…inviolate. First, I will have your total obedience, in all things. Second, you place yourself under my control, completely. Do you understand?"

Catie felt dizzy. No, she couldn't see well enough to know if she felt dizzy. Light-headed.

Disoriented. Not in full control of herself. And then it hit her: she didn't have to be in control in this room, because *he* was in control. Her job was simply to obey. Catie melted into the memory of how she'd felt when she had knelt for him in Lola's office. It was better than any role she'd ever played. It was totally freeing, because she was under his control. She was under his protection. He would take care of her.

If only this were real life.

In the dark, she smiled.

"I understand, sir," she said.

But then he flicked a switch and a single overhead lamp came on, dispelling any sense of comfort she might have had. It hung on a chain in the middle of the room, over a table and two chairs. It looked like an interrogation room from a spy movie. It would be almost funny if it weren't for one thing: the only reason to interrogate someone is if you think they have a secret.

She was going to be interrogated.

Does he know? How could he?

She forced herself to calm down. There was no way he knew. None. He would have kicked her right out of Volare immediately if he did; he wouldn't mess around with all these games, would he? He would hate her if he knew who she really was.

That thought was not comforting.

Jake walked out from behind her and went to the table. He shrugged off his fine jacket, under which he was wearing another tailored shirt, and hung the jacket on the back of the chair. He pulled the chair out and pushed the table sideways so there was room in front of it, and then he turned to look back at Catie.

He began to roll his cuffs up, exposing muscular forearms.

"It's good that you haven't moved, Catie, because I did not tell you to. You are a natural submissive, you know," he said, regarding her with that evaluative stare again. "You cannot fail, in the way you are worried about failing."

Catie tried to keep her face expressionless. She had been wrong. Nothing about this would be easy.

"Thank you, sir," she said.

Jake hitched up his slacks and sat wide-legged in the chair. His body language was unmistakable. He was in command. Except for the modern dress, he might have been a king or a conqueror or something, commanding his forces from a throne.

"Come here," he said. "And kneel."

She was glad her skirt was short enough that it didn't cause her much difficulty, but the floor in this room was hard and uncomfortable, not like the carpet in Lola's office.

"It's proper manners to kneel before me, you know," he said, like they were just having a normal conversation. "There are all sorts of things many Doms will expect you to know. Different commands, different etiquette. That they are all different strikes me as an argument for treating each encounter, each partner, with the unique respect that it or they deserve. But many Doms are idiots. I do not advise you to become involved with idiots. In any event, I don't necessarily hold with formality of manners, though in some cases I may demand it, and then I will tell you so."

Catie met his eye. "Then why am I kneeling, sir?"

"Because I like to see you down there."

He smiled wickedly at her.

"Not everything has a reason, Catie. Some things just *are*. First lesson."

"I know that one already," she said. "Sir."

Catie immediately wished she could take that back. She'd said it because she'd thought of *him*, of her attraction to him, and how it seemed to exist as its own entity in the world, its own force of nature, and she'd just instinctively told the truth about it. There was no reason for it. It simply was. It was like the way she was alone in the world, and had no one else: it simply was. Wondering why didn't change anything.

Oh God, please don't ask me what I meant.

But Jake was simply watching her with that half smile. Did he know what she'd meant? Or was he thinking of his own life?

"Good," he finally said. "Get up and sit in that other chair."

She did, glad to be out from under his stare. Maybe it would give her a chance to collect herself. Compulsive truth telling was not something she could afford to do. She couldn't lose control like that again. She had to keep focused. She *wanted* to keep focused — on *him*.

The chair itself was a simple metal frame with a metal seat. It looked grim, but wasn't particularly uncomfortable. It was neutral — she didn't feel it much, one way or the other. She supposed that was by design, too. It would certainly let her keep her mind on other sensations.

"First important question: what are your hard limits?"

She stared at him.

"I don't know."

"That is not an acceptable answer. You have been here long enough to know that."

Catie studied Jake, sitting with that relaxed sense of command, calmly looking at her with his uniquely aristocratic wildness, and realized, with both horror and elation, that she couldn't think of anything she wouldn't let him do. That was insane. It couldn't be. Yet he brought out all the darkness in her, every crazy whim or impulse she'd ever had. How could one man do that?

"I know," she said. "I can't explain it. But I don't trust myself to answer, because I don't know."

His eyes narrowed, and she heard him suck in his breath very quickly.

"Go on."

"I think I need you to help me figure them out," she said quietly. "I think it's different…with you."

"But you hardly know anything about me, Catie."

She smiled, not able to help herself. "Some things just *are*, sir."

Jake's hands closed into tight fists and his knuckles got very white, but he never stopped looking at Catie. His face was stone. Only his eyes were alive, burning with an intensity that might have frightened another woman. It didn't frighten her. It made her want more. With a start, Catie realized that she wanted to know about Jake. She wanted to know him, to be inside his head, the way she felt he'd been inside hers. More than that, she felt like she needed it. But whether it was for Brazzer or herself, she wasn't yet willing to say.

Except she was the one in the hot seat.

chapter 7

She squirmed and allowed herself to look up at him. She'd been wrong about the positioning of the light above; as he drew his own chair in, it was slightly behind his head, casting his face in shadow. He studied her for several long seconds before he seemed to come back to himself and remember they were there for a purpose.

"We begin with an interview," he said, his expression returning to normal.

"An interview, or an interrogation?" she blurted out.

Now he smiled at her, his eyes still shining. He seemed entertained, leaning back in his chair with his shirt pulled across his chest. He looked up at the light and then down at the table. "Well, it's not a subtle set-up, is it?"

Catie swallowed and tried not to look scared.

He leaned forward, watching her face carefully. "You know the club safewords, of course?"

She nodded. "Green, yellow, red. Like a traffic light."

"And you were telling the truth when you said that you trust me?"

"Yes."

"Then I wonder why you look frightened."

He didn't wait for an answer but got up and then, swiftly, walked somewhere behind her, into the dark. He didn't explain what he was doing. He didn't explain what he had meant. He just let her wait.

When he came back into the tent of light spilling down from the light hanging overhead, he carried two boxes—one black, one white—that he placed on the table in front of her. The white one was a leather chest with a lock large enough to be a suitcase. The black one was smaller, about the size of a shoebox.

"This interview has a purpose," he said. "To train you, I have to know you. I have to know what you like, what you do not like, what you think you will hate but in fact love, and why. I have to come to know you better than you know yourself in some ways."

Catie kept her expression carefully alert, maybe a little apprehensive. This was exactly what she feared: if Jake got to know her—really know her—and why she had come to Volare, she would lose everything. And yet, some part of her felt giddy, wanted to indulge in the fantasy that maybe he would get to know her, *and he'd like her*. The thought was like a little spark of warmth, flickering just out of reach. It was seductive. Tempting.

Fantasies are for children, Catie. You've got adult responsibilities.

She dragged her thoughts back to the present and shook off the comforting fantasy, reminding herself that she needed to live in reality. She needed to get biographical details about Jake, not give him her own.

"Do I get to know you?" she asked. "I mean, you brought it up. Sir."

His head jerked up, his body paused in the act of sitting down in his chair. His brows were raised in one of those expressions of genuine surprise that leaves ripples along the whole forehead, but the sudden expressiveness of his face made him look younger. She suddenly wondered what he looked like when he really laughed.

The expression faded as he sat back in his chair, replaced by that twinkle in his eye.

"The interview has rules," he continued. Apparently he would only answer her questions when he felt like it. "I will ask the questions. You will answer them with total, complete honesty. If you cannot answer a question, you will choose a card from this box." He pointed to the black one.

Catie looked at the box. It seemed somehow ominous.

"And if you do well," he said, "perhaps I will let you come."

It was the first time he'd mentioned sex. The word "come" penetrated right to her core, resurrecting the ghost of the last orgasm he'd given her. It hummed throughout her body in anticipation. He would touch her. He would do things to her. At any moment. She had to try to keep her head in the midst of all that.

"Yes, sir," she said softly.

He smiled quickly, and then his face became grim, serious. He rose from his chair with the familiar athletic grace and shoved the table aside, leaving no barrier between them. The sound of the table sliding across the floor hung in the air as he stood over her.

"Grip the seat of your chair with your hands," he said. "Do not let go unless I tell you to."

Catie felt for the edge of her seat and squeezed. She kept her eyes locked on his face as he swung his arm down, almost carelessly, and flicked open the buttons of her button down shirt in one motion.

She had picked her outfit in a kind of panic, not knowing what the dress code for this sort of thing was, and in the end she had gone with a sexy business sort of look, thinking it made her look respectable. He'd just destroyed all pretense at respectability. She felt...despoiled.

Her body tensed for him.

"You were right to wear a bra that clasps in the front," he said, looking down at her. "I would hate to cut something so fine."

With the same ease, he snapped her bra open and pushed it aside, leaving her breasts exposed. She took a deep breath, her eyes locked on Jake as she felt her nipples tighten.

He took his fill of the sight of her, then turned and opened the white leather chest. She couldn't see what was inside, but what he took out glinted in the harsh light.

"First question: do you have prior experience with BDSM?" he said.

"Yes." She was focused on his closed hand, the one that held whatever it was he'd taken out of the box.

He arched an eyebrow and circled in around her.

"I told you I required complete honesty," he said. "Complete. Anything less will be punished."

She shuddered. If he only knew. She opened her mouth to speak, but he interrupted her:

"*Complete*," he said again.

What was he getting at? She had tried some stuff, but not...

"Not like this," she said. Why was she breathing so hard? "I tried, with my ex, but he wasn't...it wasn't really his thing."

Jake was silent. Then:

"I reviewed your application after our first meeting. My understanding was that you obtained a reference from a BDSM club in Chicago."

Oh shit. She had, sort of, in that when Master Roman called to check out her application, she'd paid Danny to pretend to be the owner of a small BDSM club, small enough that no one would have heard of it, and he'd flubbed his lines, like he always did, and said Chicago. She'd never even *been* to Chicago. She'd had to pretend she'd made a mistake on the application.

"Yes, sir," she said, "I had an internship at a comedy theater that summer." Please let it have been in summer. "But I didn't really... I was never comfortable enough to fully participate, I guess."

"Why not?"

"Because of what I said before. We weren't a good fit."

"Why not with anyone else?"

She stayed silent. There hadn't been a BDSM club, of course. But it was true she'd only made half-hearted efforts. She didn't have a ready explanation.

"Was there anyone you trusted?" he asked. "Think."

Catie blinked, and told the truth, "No."

Jake reached down with both hands, a chain glittering between them, and then there was something biting down on her nipples. She looked down and saw that he'd pinched each nipple with a shining metal clamp. His fingers remained poised on the levers, gradually letting them close ever tighter around her flesh. The pain shot through her in sudden, shocking spurts, each one terminating in the nexus of sensation between her legs, where it blossomed into pleasure.

"And yet you just allowed me to put metal clamps on your nipples, and you never once moved your hands from the seat," he observed. "As ordered."

Catie was having trouble breathing. She'd never felt anything like this. Her abdominal muscles contracted in time with her short, labored breaths, and she felt sweat begin to bead on her collarbone. Her mind raced to keep up with the physical sensations that tore through her body.

"What does that feel like, Catie?"

She licked her lips. "Good."

"The pain?"

"Yes."

"Tell me more."

"Confusing. Like being tossed back and forth, and there's no more…"

She had been about to say no more room for lies. It felt like it. If she let herself fall into the sensation completely, she'd lose the strength to keep up the façade, and then she'd just be herself—who knows what she'd say. She realized that part of her *wanted* to confess, wanted to be known for what she was, and it terrified her, but the added danger heightened the physical sensation. She shook her head and said only, "It feels good."

She could feel him watching her. She kept her eyes half-lidded, trying to regain control of herself. Already she was becoming accustomed to the sensations, already she was learning to ride them, rather than be ridden by them.

"Catie," he said, and she looked up. He was watching her. That look…it felt like he could see through her, every time.

He can't, Catie. Get a grip.

"Clasp your hands behind the back of the chair."

She released her grip on the bottom of the chair, surprised to find she'd been holding on to it so hard, and did as instructed. It stretched her back, moving her breasts a little and pulling at her nipples. She sighed, and she thought she saw him grin.

Jake moved over to the white box again, and this time came around behind her chair. She heard him come close, and then there was a swath of black across her eyes.

A blindfold.

"Where did you grow up?" he asked. He tied

the blindfold tightly.

"California."

"What did your parents do?"

"My dad is—was—a real estate agent."

"Was?"

His questions were coming rapid fire, and it was hard to think about anything other than what he might be planning to do next—not being able to see put her on high physical alert, draining her mental defenses. She struggled.

"He doesn't do that anymore."

"What does he do now?"

Her tone grew sharp and brittle, like a blade of glass. "I don't know."

There was a pause. A silence, more like. She wondered if she could call "red" for the questions alone. She didn't want to, she didn't want the session to end, and yet she didn't...

She didn't want to be thinking about this.

When he finally spoke, his tone was gentler. "And your mother?"

"Dead."

"Ah."

'Ah?' 'Ah?' What the hell did that mean? Catie felt the first stirrings of anger. She was sitting blindfolded in a chair with her chest exposed, her nipples clamped, her hands clasped behind her back, and Jake was—

His voice split her thoughts.

He said, "Spread your legs."

Her belly tightened involuntarily, and her mind stopped thinking about anything other than what was coming next. Slowly, she remembered it had been a command. She spread her legs, blind to what was in front of her. All she could hear was her own rapid breathing.

Then she felt him — more than heard him — kneel between her legs. She couldn't be certain until his hands came to rest on her knees and began to push slowly up her thighs. Her mind went right back into overdrive, and for a moment, she panicked that she would lose control.

"Sir—"

His hands stopped and squeezed her legs gently.

"You do not have to be afraid. I will take care of you, if you will let me."

But that was the problem: she did have to be afraid. She had to be terrified. She couldn't let him take care of her, not without feeling terrible, not without betraying him even more completely, and not without risking...

"Just tell me the truth."

And his hands resumed their advance up the length of her legs, scrambling her thoughts once again.

"What did you want to be when you grew up?"

"What?"

"You heard me," he said, and his thumbs reached down the insides of her thighs and hooked under the hem of her skirt. "What did you dream of being when you were little?"

Each beat of her heart, perfectly in time as his hands slipped a little farther, pushing her skirt up her legs and defining a new border — a border she desperately wanted him to cross.

"A Roman general," she said, blushing immediately. She hadn't meant to say that. It was completely, one hundred percent true, but it was also so ridiculous that she had never told anyone.

There was a pause.

"Really?" he said. "Why?"

She nodded, blushing furiously. "Yes. I read about them. In my dad's study, there were these fake leather bound books. I mean the leather was fake, not...They were always so smart and wily, and then they came home, and they were heroes, even if only for a little while. They'd *earned* it. At least the ones who made it into the books."

"Well," he said, pushing her skirt up to her waist, "some of them. The Romans didn't necessarily share all of our values, but they believed in rewards and punishment. As do I."

Catie had been prepared to feel completely humiliated by that admission, by that profoundly weird insight into her strange mind and lonely childhood, and waited for it to arrive. When it didn't—when no embarrassment was forthcoming, when she didn't feel completely foolish—she realized it was because he'd made it seem...interesting.

She was on the verge of thanking him when she felt his hands on her thighs again. She stopped breathing when she felt him pull her underwear away and heard the *snip* of a pair of scissors. He was cutting her underwear off of her. Soon she'd be completely helpless, completely unable to hide, and then she might lose everything. And she didn't have the strength to tell him to stop, because she wanted him, again, wanted whatever he wanted to do to her.

"Please," she said, and it sounded almost like

she might cry. "Please, no more questions."

His hands gripped the back of her buttocks and pulled her suddenly forward, near the edge of the seat.

"You're afraid," he said. "I told you not to be afraid."

"I can't help it."

"What are you afraid of?"

She felt his lips on the skin of her inner thigh. She'd never had a man talk to her while he was down there, never even imagined how that would be, had always just closed her eyes and took the physical sensation for what it was. It had never been so intimate as it was in a fake interrogation room with a man who had blindfolded her. A man who she had to hide from. A man whose last name she didn't even know.

"I'm afraid if you know me, you won't..."

But she couldn't finish.

"Tell me your name," she begged.

He didn't speak, but covered her clit with his mouth. She recoiled from the sudden intensity, overwhelmed, her circuits blown. He held on to her and pulled her closer, and with a jerk, he pushed her chair back until it was balanced on two legs, angling her up to him, his one hand holding it steady in the back. How strong was he? His questions had come fast and hard, had been meant to disorient her, knock the truth out of her, and now his tongue came slow and strong, meant to coax...what? The question rose to the surface in her mind, fringed with panic, and then was sucked back down, obliterated by the sensation of his tongue lathing in tender circles around the border of her most sensitive area.

Her fingernails dug into her own skin as she fought not to bring her hands around, to grip the hair on his head and pull him into her. She wasn't physically bound, but she could not move. She didn't understand it. She didn't understand anything that was going on inside her body, and when she felt the first rumblings of an orgasm barreling towards her, again her first instinct was to fight it or flee or *something*. She couldn't lose control, couldn't...

But she did.

He tore it out of her, relentless, sucking on her clit until she came for him, screaming, again.

Something clanged, and a jolt rocked her body, pulling the clamps at her nipples harder. It took Catie a moment to realize it was her chair, coming back to rest on the ground. She had been fully prepared to accept that it was internal, an aftershock, some other new thing. The clamps were gently removed and her nipples began to fill with a rush of blood. She whimpered slightly from the pain of it, the way a leg hurts when it's been asleep, and then her blindfold was removed and she saw Jake kneeling between her legs, his thumbs pressing softly into her nipples, massaging them slowly.

"You've done very well," he said.

"At what?" she mumbled. She still quivered, her knees shaking against his ribs.

He smiled.

"So far I've discovered how you react to various stimuli and peppered you with exploratory questions in a way designed to disorient so you could not lie. You did very well, Catie. I will be able to train you."

Now she opened her eyes fully and tried to sit up straight, but she couldn't get the proper leverage with her hands still clasped behind her back. Instead she glared at him with the aggression of a woman who is overcompensating.

"Why do you think I would lie?" she demanded.

Jake's eyes held her own, but seemed, for a moment, far away. She needed him to be close to her and she needed to hide from him all at once, and because it was impossible, she felt herself starting to get angry.

"Everybody lies," he said, and rose.

She had no answer for that.

He reached down to cup her cheek and tilt her face up to his. "If I had asked you if you enjoyed bondage, I am not sure you would have been truthful, even to yourself. You think you like to fight. And you do, at times. But you also have kept your hands clasped behind your back this entire time, without the aid of physical restraint. We have learned something new."

Catie forgot to be angry for a moment, and instead was bewildered. She had. She still *was*.

"You may release your hands now."

She brought them back quickly to her lap and found that they were trembling. Jake had been inside her head again. Despite her best efforts, despite the fact that she had her own job to do, despite everything that made it a terrible idea. He'd been inside her head because she'd let him in. Burning with recrimination, she pulled her skirt back down and moved to close her shirt.

"No," he said sharply. "Leave it open. I like to look at you."

Catie paused. No, she hesitated. There was a moment where her hands hung in the air, and they could go either way, when she was deciding whether to obey. It was only that he had come so close to her again, had been inside her, even if he hadn't...

No, she could do this. She let her hands fall to her sides and felt herself begin to flood with warmth again, even so soon after coming for him.

His thumb brushed her cheek, a gesture of approval, and without thinking, she turned and took it into her mouth. She sucked on it and let her tongue slide over it before nipping it with her teeth.

She heard his intake of breath as she let his thumb go and she looked up at him, feeling somehow triumphant. He was rigidly motionless, his face on fire.

Stiffly, he said, "There is one last question."

chapter 8

"Who would you call if you were in trouble?" Jake asked.

Catie blinked. She must have misheard.

"What?"

"Who would you call if you were in trouble? If you needed help — if something went wrong here. Someone you could trust to come to your aid, no matter what the situation," he said.

He was still looking at her. Catie wanted to look anywhere else but up at him. She cast about wildly, looking for something, anything. She thought she had been prepared for his questions, she thought she could rely on her improvisation skills, but now her mind was blank. It wouldn't allow her to think about this. Her eyes fell on the black box, still on the table, and she almost wanted to cry with relief.

"You said I could choose a card from the box if I couldn't answer," she said, her words coming very quickly. "I choose the box. I'll choose a card."

"No."

His fingers threaded through her hair, and she remembered the last time they'd been together and looked over at the table, wondering. But he wanted her to look at him.

"Not for this question. This question, you must answer."

"I don't want to."

"You must."

"You can't make me."

She cringed. She hadn't meant to sound like a child. She hadn't meant to be reminded of her own pathetic situation. Volare was an escape from that, it was her way out, it was a place where she could be someone else, not the poor little rich girl who wasn't rich anymore and whose family didn't give a shit about her.

That was it. She wasn't just drawing a line in the sand. She didn't want to answer because she knew the answer, and it was terrible.

"Catie," he said softly.

She looked back up at him again and pretended she didn't have tears welling up in her eyes.

"Is it because there isn't anyone?" he asked.

He'd know if she lied this time. He'd know, and he'd know she could lie about anything. And yet, admitting it would make it real. She hadn't thought about how often she lied to herself; about how often she'd pretended that her father was about to come around, that she'd hear from him soon, that it would all turn out to be a mistake. But now someone else had asked. Now Jake had guessed, and she couldn't lie any longer, not even to herself. She wasn't a coward. She plunged ahead.

"Yes," she said. "There isn't anyone. I'm alone."

He looked at her for what felt like a long time. Several times, she thought he was about to say something, but he never did. He just stood there, stroking her cheek, smoothing her hair, watching her with eyes that had gone soft.

Finally, he said, "Thank you for telling me, Catie. I will arrange for something. Stay here. I will be back shortly."

And he walked out of the room.

Catie was slightly stunned. She didn't pretend to know so much about Volare and the rules and expectations surrounding a training session, but she knew people, and she knew he shouldn't have *left*. He'd just made her answer all these questions, he'd just made her answer *that* question, he'd made her come again—he shouldn't leave her. He should…

Well, what did she want from him? He'd said he didn't get attached. He wasn't "built" that way. But then he got so close to her, so close to something hard and sensitive deep inside her, a place where she was bruised all over, something she'd been able to block out, emotionally, until he came along and demanded access to it. Something he made more real by asking those questions. No, she didn't have anyone. She was alone. No one wanted her. Thanks for pointing it out.

And now the person she'd felt closest to was someone who said he wouldn't get attached. Someone who left her here, after all that.

"Screw this," she said, and dressed herself.

She felt her old defenses growing back, like a scab. She had to remember why she was here. It helped to think of it as a tactical diversion, part of a larger strategy. What would a Roman general do?

She eyed the room critically. She might as well learn something.

That's when she saw his jacket, still hanging on the back of his chair. Even if she wasn't worth anything to anyone else, she could prove she was worth *something*. She could do what she came here to do: file her story and support what remained of her family.

She walked over to it, and hesitated for just a moment. Even with everything that had just happened, even with the way he'd refused to tell her his name, even with everything she needed to do to save her grandmother, there was something in her that was repelled at the idea of going through a man's wallet.

"Get over it, creampuff," she said, and rifled quickly through the pockets.

It was a simple, fine leather wallet, but expensive. She could tell from the quality of the leather. But she could tell he was rich from the suit he was wearing today, and from the fact that his clothes were always tailored. Many of the members of Volare had money; it was no surprise.

His name, however, was a surprise. A shock, in fact.

She read off of his driver's license twice. Then she read it again.

"*That* Jacob Jayson?" she said aloud.

"Yes," Jake said behind her. "*That* Jacob Jayson."

Oh shit.

Oh. Shit.

Slowly, she turned. There was no point in hiding what she'd been doing. She was still holding his wallet and his driver's license. And he'd heard her say his name. His name that he very obviously wanted to protect, and for very good reason.

Jake—Jacob—stood in the middle of the doorway, his hand still resting on the doorknob. His face had lost all expressiveness, which was somehow worse. She expected him to be angry, upset, betrayed. She could have responded naturally to that, could have fought back. Could have reacted, could have improvised. But he surveyed her with the cold calculation of a machine, and now she knew what it was really like to be lonely in this room. The anger she'd felt when he'd left flooded in to fill the vacancy.

"You wouldn't tell me," she said. "It wasn't fair. You had just asked me...you had just demanded that I tell you things that were so private, and you wouldn't even tell me your *name*. How could I trust you?"

He was silent.

"You *deserved* it," she said hotly.

At the snap of her words Jake's head tilted back, as though he'd been struck, and a flicker of human emotion lit up his face. Catie was afraid to move, to speak, to breathe, for fear of what that emotion would be. She herself was torn between righteous indignation at the fact that he really did deserve it, and guilt because, well, that's not the only reason she'd done it. And then Jake stepped forward, and she saw him more clearly. She saw that he was lit up with…

Lust?

"You play games, Catie," he said, closing the door behind him. "You play games to provoke. I do not know why, as of yet. But let's find out what kind of response you crave."

What I crave…

His tone sent shivering sparks shooting through her body until her skin tingled all over. She already knew what it meant.

"You must be disciplined," he said, and pulled the table across the floor with a harsh screech, back to the center of the room. Catie stared at it, wide-eyed. *Disciplined.* The word itself sent her blood rushing to her core. She was feeling lightheaded again, her pulse throbbing in every sensitive part of her, her hearing dulled.

"Disciplined?" she asked. Her throat was dry.

"I won't call it punishment yet," Jake said. "That remains to be determined. But you promised your obedience, Catie. Now obey. Bend over and lay your forearms flat on the table."

This. *This.* This was the energy she remembered from Lola's office, when he'd dragged her up by her hair…

She walked over to the table in a kind of trance. The anticipation was better than any drug she'd ever tried back in her wild teenage years. Every nerve felt alive and primed and happy, ready to sing out in a chorus of sensation. Even pain.

She bent over and put her forearms flat on the table. She felt hot between her legs, and that familiar peace came over her as all thought disappeared from her mind, leaving only her desire behind. She wanted him. She wanted his domination. She needed relief—from lying, from the interview. From doing things she knew to be wrong. From everything.

"Yes, sir," she whispered.

His fingers danced up the backs of her naked legs, and she sighed. He grabbed the hem of her skirt and yanked it over her buttocks, so rapidly she thought she heard the fabric rip. That small sound gave her chills.

Her underwear was still lying ruined on the floor somewhere. He'd be able to see how wet she was for him all over again. She listened hard for the sound of a zipper, *wanted* to hear the sound of his zipper, was aching to feel him inside her again, but instead—

"Oh, I'm not going to fuck you," he said behind her. "You don't deserve to be fucked again yet."

And then she felt his first blow.

It was his hand, just his open palm, expertly placed at the juncture where her buttocks curved into her legs so that it stung in rippling waves that shook her flesh and made her ache for more. Her breasts swung forward and her sore nipples brushed the table through her shirt, and she gasped.

He spanked her again and again, until she could feel the wetness spill down her inner thighs, until she thought she would come just from the impact. She moaned, and started to arch toward him, and she thought, for just a moment, she thought he might…

He grunted and put his hand between her legs, as if just to remind her she was still under his control. She did not move, held still at the precipice. Her body needed to come.

"No," he said. His voice was hoarse, and she thought she heard it tremble. "This is your punishment, Catie. If you want to be trained by me — if you want to be trained at Volare — you will not come again without my permission."

She turned her head to protest, but his hand kept her locked in place. Not without his permission? The idea made her so hot, and so frustrated. She made a fist with her hand and slammed it down on the table.

He laughed, and his thumb penetrated her, almost carelessly. "I can always decide to make it more challenging."

She breathed heavily. "Yes, you could," she said. "Sir."

She didn't know what wild impulse made her call his bluff — maybe the same one that sent her across the country to infiltrate Volare, or that got her to go through his wallet — but she shouldn't have done it.

"Don't move," he said, and removed his hand. She heard the white chest open once more, and she closed her eyes. No matter what it was, she wouldn't be allowed to come — not unless he said so.

"These will make it harder. But when I do allow you to come," he said, "Well, you will have earned it. In this way, perhaps you will learn control."

"What —"

His hand came into view at her side. It held two textured silver balls, about the size of golf balls, connected by a length of string. He rolled them around in his palm, and she could hear something rattling around inside the balls.

"Ben-wa balls," he said. "Spread your legs."

Her eyes widened. He was going to put those inside her? Both of them?

"Catie."

She spread her legs and focused on the scratched metal surface of the table. The first ball was cold, and felt impossibly large pushed up against her flesh. She whimpered, and then his finger was there, working around the edges, dipping into her wetness again and again. Still, the ball stretched her until she thought she couldn't go any further, her head dipping down to the table, and then suddenly it was in, sucked into her like it belonged there.

It felt impossibly strange. Full.

And there was another one.

The second ball entered her with greater ease, but she was sure she couldn't hold them both. She was wrong. Jake pushed the second ball in after the first, filling her beyond what she'd thought possible. Then he tugged at the string, pulling them back against her closed entrance, and she cried out. It felt...*incredible*.

"Stand up," he ordered.

She pushed herself off the table and stopped midway, shocked by the sudden vibrations that reverberated through her. Whatever it was inside the ben-wa balls, it moved whenever she did, jingling like a pair of silent, vibrating bells.

"You will wear these Mondays, Wednesdays, and Fridays," he said. "You will have to work to keep them in. Every time you move, you will think of me. You will think of the promise you have made to me. You will think of obedience. You will think of whatever orders I have given you. And," he said as he turned her around to face him, her skin flushed, her body rattled by what was going on inside her, "you will remember not to come."

She looked at him with utter dismay. It was impossible. She wanted to come *now*. She had no idea how she was supposed to walk even to the other side of the room without losing control.

Jake—Jacob, he was Jacob now, too; it fit, now that she knew—Jacob smiled slightly, but his eyes were once again aflame. She couldn't turn away. She would think of him every time she moved. He was inside her now, all the time, in more ways than one.

For just a moment, he seemed as transfixed as she was.

"Yes, sir," she finally said.

He cleared his throat.

"We have another session next Saturday," he said. "See that you figure out how to show me what you've been hiding by then."

Catie met his gaze. So he knew she was hiding something. But so was he. And she would find out what.

"I will, sir," she said levelly. "You can be sure that I will."

chapter 9

Jake watched the boy until he was sure.

He'd taken his usual car service down to Stephan's House, and given the vagaries of the neighborhood, the car had begun its usual loop around the one-way streets so that it could deliver Jake to the front door. The weather was, once again, horrible. A sort of dirty, cold slush fell from the sky, blown about in sudden, angry crosswinds.

Which was why it was so unusual to see someone hanging around outside.

Jake had recognized him at once. His stance. Posture and gait were always identifying; they were said to be as unique as fingerprints. And he remembered where he'd seen the boy before: at one of the free dinners at Stephan's House. It happened to coincide with one of Jake's own failed attempts to engage with the people he tried to help; periodically, even Jake forgot what he was and tried to become more. It never worked, but that was beside the point. Even then, Jake had noticed that this boy had not been interested in the counseling services, a bed for the night, or even the free food. That was what had struck him as odd: no matter how distrustful of authority, no matter how traumatized, no matter how unreachable, they always took the food. Hunger was a primal need that overruled every other psychological ailment.

But this boy had been more interested in the other kids who'd come in for help. The other drug addicted, homeless, abused, wayward kids. Jake had seen him move easily between tables, bending to whisper into an ear here, sitting to chat there. At the time, Jake hadn't been able to figure it out.

Now that he saw the boy on the corner, in this weather, displaying quite the work ethic, he knew. He knew the boy had been looking for customers that night. The boy was a drug dealer.

"I'll get out here," Jake said to his driver. He reached for the account slip and signed it, never taking his eyes off the boy.

The slush had turned to little needles of ice in the time he'd spent in his comfortable car, and he squinted into the wind as he stuffed his scarf into his overcoat and pulled on his gloves. He managed to make it across the avenue without stepping in any icy puddles, and the momentum of rushing across the street against traffic carried him into the next block without much thought. The boy watched him approach with stony silence.

Jake was only a few feet away now. He could

see that the boy was older than he'd thought, just small. Perhaps malnourished in his youth. A young man, thin, rat-faced, angry. Jake had expected to be angry himself—he *was* angry, at being deceived and used—but what he was most conscious of now, standing in front of the kid, was how warm and comfortable his own clothes were compared to the shitty jacket that the drug dealer wore.

He couldn't be a very good drug dealer, then.

"What the fuck you want, man?"

Jake looked at him levelly. "This is your territory? This corner?"

"I don't know what you're fucking talking about." He was nervous. Jake didn't look like a cop, but he didn't look like he belonged where he was, either.

"Yes, you do," Jake said. "This is your territory. Fine. I could call the police. I could have a squad car sitting right here, every day, forever. You don't know this about me, but I am one of the few people in this city who can call the mayor and make that happen. And I can have you chased down like a criminal. I can bring the full *fucking* weight of the law down on your head with one phone call. So I suggest you pay attention to what I am about to say."

He had the dealer's full attention. Good. Jake took a deep breath.

"That place you came to looking for customers—Stephan's House—that is *my* territory. You do not darken its doors ever again looking for trade. You do not go there looking for customers. If you do, so help me God…" Jake broke off, quelling the anger rising within him. Anger wouldn't help.

"But," he went on, "that's where you should go if you ever want help. Or food. Or a place to sleep. Whatever."

Jake dug a card out of his pocket and held it out, doing his best to protect it from the sleet. The dealer stared at it like it was a deadly weapon.

"You for real?" he finally said.

"Yes," Jake said. "Take the card, and don't give me a reason to call the police."

The dealer took it with a look that Jake had come to know well: the intent to deceive. It didn't matter. You did what you could.

Jake kept telling himself that, over and over again, all the way back to Stephan's House, as though maybe if he only said it enough times, it would become true. He needed a day in which it seemed like the myriad people he tried to help actually welcomed his intervention. In which it seemed like it mattered what he did. In which it seemed like the entire world was not out to deceive, manipulate, or misuse what he had to offer.

He entered Stephan's House and made his way up to his office via the back stairs, not wanting to inflict his current mood upon anyone else until he'd had time to recuperate with at least one cup of coffee. He opened his office door with relief, looking forward to being alone, only to find that his office was already occupied.

Eileen Corrigan was sitting comfortably in one chair.

And Catie Roberts was in the other.

Jake stood, frozen in the motion of taking off his

scarf, and stared at the two women who currently occupied most of his thoughts.

How long have they been here?

What have they talked about?

Eileen sat there and smirked at him, while Catie tried to hide her face behind that beautiful dark hair. The intrusion of Catie into this part of his life was…he didn't know what it was, not yet. He had called around, after their first session, as much as he'd enjoyed it, unable to completely banish the most paranoid thoughts from his mind. His mother had seen to it that Jake's natural suspicious tendencies were honed to a fine, deadly point, the sort of thing guaranteed to keep most people at arm's length. He could hear her now: *They'll only be after your money. Never trust them.* It's what had counted as a heart to heart in his mother's house, and no matter how hard he tried to be a different sort of person, the words had seeped into his bones. He would always be able to hear their echo.

So when he'd called around to various departments at City Community College and had been unable to determine who Catie was working with on her thesis, he had not been comforted.

And now she was here, in the part of his life that dealt with the most personal, private things, sitting and chatting with the woman who knew more about those things than anyone else still living.

"Aren't you gonna say hi?" Eileen asked. "What's the matter with you? You look like you're gonna barf."

Jake finished unwinding his scarf and took advantage of the moment to rein in his wilder thoughts.

"Hello, Eileen," he said, nodding, and made his way around to his desk. There, he fixed his stare on Catie. "I see you've met Catie."

Eileen smiled, a little too slyly. "That I have."

Catie still wouldn't look at him.

"Catie, who is your advisor at City?"

That appeared to grab her attention. Her head snapped up, her blue eyes wide. "What?"

"You heard me. Who is your thesis advisor?"

Eileen looked back and forth between them as Catie's cheeks reddened. Catie cocked her head in a fair approximation of righteous indignation and looked Jake right in the eye.

"Are you checking up on me?"

"Answer the question."

"I'm supposed to trust you, but you don't trust me? What kind of bull—"

"Hey," Eileen broke in. "Jacob, what's the matter with you? That's polite?"

Jake shook his head. Eileen's voice—it was a voice from the past. The rough but attentive mothering she'd always directed at Stephan, the kind of thing Jake had always wished, secretly, might be directed at him. If only he were important enough, if only he were worth it. He'd known he wasn't welcome back then by how little Eileen cared about anything he did. And now she cared about his manners?

He was dazed.

Eileen looked sideways at Catie and said, "I thought you said you two weren't involved."

"We don't have a personal relationship, no," Catie said icily, daring Jake to contradict her. He couldn't help but notice that her eyes were beautiful when she was angry. And he couldn't help but admire the way she wielded his own words back at him. *Not a personal relationship.* "I'm here to help with the fundraising for the expansion project."

"What?" He was stunned.

"I thought you were footing the bill yourself, Jake. You didn't tell me you needed fundraising." Eileen looked hurt. Worried? Jake couldn't tell. It was as if every person in his life had been replaced by an alternate version of themselves, designed to confuse and disorient him. The notion of Eileen Corrigan being concerned for his wellbeing would have been confusing enough; Eileen Corrigan in the presence of the woman who may or may not be plotting against him, against Volare, and who he'd fantasized about just this morning *anyway*, was mind-bending.

Jake shook his head again and rubbed at his eyes. It did not help.

"I don't need help with fundraising," he said slowly. "Catie, please be so kind as to explain what you are talking about."

"Roman sent me," Catie said, her jaw set. She looked warily at Eileen, as though unsure of how much to say. "He said he's going to be my mentor, and that I should work with Lola on the benefit."

Roman.

Jake had forgotten that he'd said yes to the Volare Valentine's benefit going to Stephan's House. He had been distracted, if he remembered correctly, at the time—distracted by Catie, as he almost always seemed to be lately. The benefit would mean that he could begin plans on the next expansion concurrently without moving more money around, which would mean more staff and more services, and sooner rather than later. And it would mean a gloss of legitimacy for the charity if the biggest names in the city were known to donate. It was an unambiguously good thing.

Roman's interference was not so unambiguously good.

Jake remembered going to talk with Roman when Catie had admitted she had no one to call, no one to rely on if she got in trouble. It was an unacceptable state of affairs for a trainee. Training was an intense experience; a support network was necessary. Roman had said he would take care of it, and Jake had believed him — he believed he'd find Catie an appropriate mentor. He had not anticipated that Roman would step into the role himself.

He didn't like it.

He told himself that his own discomfort was most likely because of the things Roman knew about him, and not because of anything having to do with Catie, but the twinge in his gut was…new. Like so many things having to do with Catie. He remembered when he'd returned from speaking to Roman, he'd found Catie going through his wallet. And she'd shot back at him: *you deserved it.*

She had been right. More to the point, he had *felt* — rather than simply understood — *why* she was right.

Another new thing.

Now he felt uneasy.

He looked up to find Catie looking just as uneasy. No, she looked miserable. Wretched. But why should she? Just because he was behaving badly?

"Ok," Eileen said, clapping her hands together to break the silence. "I came in to see how you were doing, Jakey, but they have stuff for me to do downstairs, so I'll let you get back to whatever it is you need to do, all right?"

"Do you work with the kids?" Catie asked Eileen, looking suddenly interested.

Jake held his breath. He watched Eileen pause, only just, and her eyes close, just a beat too long to be a blink. He watched Catie slowly realize something had gone wrong, something she couldn't identify. He watched Eileen open her eyes and smile valiantly.

"No, dear, I just stuff envelopes and whatever else they give me. I don't have the training for that kinda thing." Eileen gathered her things efficiently, quickly, without looking at either of them. "I'll just leave you two to work out how you're not involved. Jakey, I'll see you later," she said, only a little too cheerfully, and bustled out of the room without waiting for a reply.

There was a silence.

"What did I say?" Catie finally asked. Her expression was...sad. Genuinely sad. At the idea that she might have inadvertently hurt a woman she'd only just met. She looked like she felt Eileen's pain herself, no matter how hard Eileen tried to shield them both from it, no matter how much of a stranger Eileen was to her. Jake stared at her, trying to work out what that must be like.

"She works here because her son died," Jake said. "If there had been a place like this, maybe he

94

wouldn't have."

Jake did not add: *If I had been different, maybe he wouldn't have.*

"Oh God," Catie said, turning to look over her shoulder, as though her sympathy could follow Eileen down the stairs. "Do you think…no, I mean, I know it can't help for me to talk to her. I just thought…she seems so easy to talk to…"

She is, if she doesn't hate you, Jake thought, and then admonished himself for it. This was not a good time to wallow in past resentments.

"I feel terrible," Catie said softly.

"You couldn't have known," he said, wanting to get past the whole incident. "Now tell me what it is you think you're doing here."

Immediately he regretted challenging her. It only brought out that flashing fight in her that he'd found so attractive. It only reminded him of things that were not appropriate for the time and place.

She straightened her back, which unfortunately had the effect of pushing out her breasts under that thin merino sweater, and said, "I told Roman I was in school, and he decided I'm supposed to write some copy for the Valentine's Benefit catalog. Lola said I'd need to do a tour of Stephan's House to get a feel for it."

Jake laughed. "Did they tell you what the benefit *is*? What kind of catalog it is?"

"No," Catie said, somewhat deflated for not being in on all the details. "I'm just writing the parts about Stephan's House."

What a relief. And what a disaster. That this woman should make him feel so uncomfortable, that she should be so suspicious, that she should be involved in the two things he held most dear — no, it was a farce.

"I suggest you give me a tour," she said. "And then I will be out of your hair, don't worry."

Oh, but you won't. He realized then, looking up at Catie's stubborn, angry face, at the way she was so invested in how he would reply, at the way she had *expectations* for how he would behave — and, perhaps even more so, realizing that he had his own expectations, and that he had not been quite himself since catching her in Lola's office — he realized that this had already become disastrously personal.

He had violated his one rule — not to allow a trainee to get attached — and he had done it in the one instance in which he could not immediately extricate himself because of the risk of exposure for Volare. And, perhaps even more unforgivably, he had done it for the worst possible reason: because Catie appeared to let him feel something new. But novelty was not enough of a reason to expose her to this; a leopard didn't just suddenly change its spots, and Jake was no closer to being a normal human being now than he had been five years ago. He was no more capable of giving normal human beings the affection they deserved than he had been then, and it was abominable to allow Catie to believe that he was. It could only result in terrible things.

And yet, he could not simply cut her loose. There was the ongoing question of her thesis, and the many things she already knew.

There was only one solution. He would have to be so horrible that no woman in her right mind could feel anything for him. He would have to be an utter bastard, for her own good.

"Are you wearing the ben-wa balls?" he asked suddenly.

She blushed, and looked briefly around, even though they were alone. "It's Tuesday," she said. "You said Monday, Wednesday, and Friday."

"So it is. Did you have fun Googling me over the weekend?"

Now her blush intensified. "I already knew most of it."

This surprised him. He had expected her to be too embarrassed to admit that she might have looked into his past.

"And no," she said, the heat returning to her face, "I did *not* enjoy it. It was just sad."

Jake felt as though he'd been struck. He was used to the tabloid sensationalism, to eager, salacious, predatory gossip. He was prepared for her to regard him as source of entertainment; he was prepared to see her revel in *schadenfreude*. He was not prepared for Catie to *sympathize* with him.

"Don't pity me," he said quietly.

"Who said I was? You're a freaking Jayson."

That he was, with all that it meant. Jake took a deep breath. Fine. A tour. If she wanted to see what the Jaysons were truly like beneath the veneer of wealth and breeding, he would show her. And by the end, she couldn't possibly be enamored of him.

"Follow me," he said.

chapter 10

Jake began with the administrative pool on the opposite side of the top floor, mostly to give himself a chance to think. Catie was gleefully and immediately swarmed by the energetic volunteers and paid professionals who ran his charity for him, as he knew she would be. Jake suspected Eileen had hinted that he and Catie were dating, and too many of the grandmothers who volunteered their time wanted to see him "settled down," for some reason, and so Catie had been taken well in hand.

Which was annoying, but bought him some time. He had not thought through the idea of tour. He'd never had to *give* a tour; one of the perks of funding a charity entirely by yourself was that you never had to worry about impressing donors.

The trouble was, once you got down past the top

floor, there were privacy issues. Issues of respect, and dignity. He didn't particularly want to ask any of the residents who were trying to get clean and get their lives back on track if they'd be comfortable giving an interview.

Here, would you like to bare your soul at its lowest moment for the benefit of a charity catalog?

No. That was awful.

He didn't have a solution.

"Well, I have been officially educated about how New York City regulations suck, and about how much food restaurants throw away on a regular basis," Catie said, walking over with a bit of a dazed expression. "But I think the rest might have just…gone in one ear and out the other."

Jake grinned, in spite of himself. "Did they talk all at once?"

"Yes," she said, smiling back. "Mostly about you."

It was as though they'd forgotten to fight. She was lovely when she smiled.

Jake was the first to snap out of it.

"There is a problem I hadn't anticipated," he said. "I've never given a tour for a reason. I can't violate the residents' privacy just for your convenience."

"It's actually not all that convenient," she said dryly. He deserved that. "What do you do when someone comes to you for help? You give them a kind of tour, right, so they know what the expectations are?"

She wasn't looking him in the eye anymore. It was very noticeable.

"Yes," he said slowly. "In fact, we do. But we

call it an orientation. We find it eases people through the transition and into a sense of community."

"Give me the orientation," she said, looking up at him with grim determination. "Pretend I have no place to go and need help."

Catie held her chin high and didn't move when a strand of hair fell in her face. There was something there, something behind this. He remembered suddenly very well what she'd looked like when she'd admitted that she had no one to call if she were in trouble. She'd looked like this. Brave.

Jake stepped back, trying to identify, once more, what this new feeling was. He thought he had it, finally: he felt out of his depth. Always, with Catie, he inevitably felt out of his depth. If it were anyone else, he would have pointed out that this, too, was not entirely appropriate—unless Catie truly did feel she had nowhere to go, and was in need of help. But somehow, looking at her, like this, reminding him so much of the previous week, he did not like to think of the answer to that question, and instead found himself nodding along.

"All right," he said.

Keep focused, Jake.

He was failing miserably at driving her away from him. Not that he was particularly charming her, either, but he was too disoriented to do much of anything purposefully. This was another new feeling, and it was perhaps the polar opposite of the blissful control he normally felt as a dominant.

He opened a door for her and he smelled her perfume as she walked by. He was gripped by a desire for her then. Not just a desire for her, but for the known, elegant space of a domination scene, with *her*. BDSM had been the way he found he could most approach normalcy, the closest he could come to human expressions of love and intimacy; that's what the act of domination, of controlling another's reactions and sensations, was to him. It was only way he knew to get close. And with her, it had been...it had been as though he were no longer leading, and neither was she; there was something bigger than both of them, and he forgot, for once, how apart he was from everything.

No, that was ridiculous. It had been twice. Two encounters. This was simply more evidence that he could not be trusted to keep her at arm's length. And if she had the sort of sensitivity he'd seen her feel for Eileen, if she felt that way about everything, he could hardly avoid hurting her.

He must do better.

"Which Roman general did you want to be?" he asked as they waited for the elevator down to the main floors. He put a little bit of sneer in his voice, and hated himself for it.

That threw her. From her breathing, he could tell she was thinking about the circumstances under which she'd told him about that. *Perhaps a misstep.*

"None in particular," she said. "I wanted to be...my own."

"I thought you'd made that up," he said, satisfied to have been proven right.

She turned on him, but she didn't look angry. Just amused.

"You thought I made up a childhood desire to

be a Roman general? Really? Why on Earth would anyone do that?"

He shrugged, smiled. "Many people like to pretend at familiarity with the classics. It makes them feel cultured."

She laughed. She *laughed*.

"Yeah, my dad was one of those. Hence the books with the fake leather binding. But I read them, because I thought he was really into it. So I talked to him about Pompey or Agrippa and he looked at me like I'd grown a third arm, and eventually I figured it out and tried to talk to him about other things. But what that weirdo education *did* give me," she said, jamming her finger into the elevator button again, "was the ability to tell when someone is pushing a weak offensive as a last, desperate defense."

He said nothing. The elevator pinged open, and Catie walked inside.

"Are you done with that now?" she said, holding the door open. "Because I'd like to start the orientation."

It was at that point that Jake felt he might have gone some way towards convincing her not to feel anything for him, though not in the way he'd intended. Yet another new experience, courtesy of Catie Roberts: feeling like a total ass.

He guided her through the rest of the building in a state of stunned silence, all the while trying very hard not to notice the curves under that sweater, nor to think about the look she'd flashed him, and what that might have been like in a scene. Thinking about sex—any kind of sex—in this building made him feel like a terrible person. And he could not be around Catie without thinking about sex.

Luckily, today was not a particularly busy day. There weren't any scheduled group therapy sessions, and he'd forgotten that most of the residents were on a field trip to Chelsea Piers.

"This is an empty building," Catie said.

"It isn't normally. And I won't let you into the dormitory areas," he said. "Look, usually it's quite busy. This is one of the main recreation areas, where the residents can hopefully relax and socialize."

She looked around at the well-used ping-pong table, the comfortable looking couches, and the collection of DVDs strewn about in front of the television.

"So these are all runaways? Kids at risk?" she asked.

"Most of them, yes."

"LGBT kids who've been kicked out, drug addicts, abused minors?"

"You seem well-versed."

"Actors aren't the most stable bunch. Plus, I used to volunteer." She was quiet, her fingers pulling at a hole where the stuffing had started to come through the back of a couch. Then, "Suicidal?"

He kept his voice as even as possible. "Yes."

"How do you manage to avoid the whole social services thing?"

"We have a special pilot program accreditation," he said.

"Family connections come in handy, huh?"

He rolled his shoulders, as if trying to shrug the

association off. "Sometimes," he said. "Sometimes not."

"Well," she said, slapping the back of the couch, "this was educational. Where's the ladies' room?"

He pointed at the door on the other side of the room, and off she went. Catie had so succeeded in disorienting him that she was gone for a full fifteen minutes before he noticed that something might be wrong. Catie didn't strike him as a woman who loitered in bathrooms for the fun of it. And she was by herself.

Which was why it was doubly odd that, when he moved to knock on the door, he heard a muffled voice.

And he heard crying.

Under normal circumstances, Jake would have enough presence of mind not to walk into a women's bathroom. He was not equipped to deal with the human side of Stephan's House; he knew he would never be anyone's shoulder to cry on, nor would he be the understanding face who convinced a wary teen to trust again. His role, his usefulness in this world, lay in what he could build with the money and the gifts he'd been given. He could build Stephan's House, but he could not make it a place that helped people. He had to find others to do that. And he had accepted that about himself, long ago, and so Jake was not the first one to respond when any of the residents was in crisis. He was not the first one to respond when *anyone* was in crisis.

But he heard tears, and he thought it was Catie in there, crying. And he didn't think. He simply opened the door.

Catie was there, but she wasn't crying. She sat next to a painfully thin young woman with stringy, oil-darkened blonde hair who was crying quietly. There were scratch marks on the blonde girl's arm, raised welts where she'd gauged at herself with something.

Only Catie looked up. The girl still continued to cry, oblivious. He hadn't made much of a sound as he came in. Catie waited for him, looking at him, wanting him to do something, only he couldn't think what. And now he stood there, open mouthed, gaping like an idiot, as he watched Catie turn her attention back to the girl in trouble. It was like watching the beam from a lighthouse whip around in a storm and settle on the place where it was needed. What he remembered most as he backed out of the room, careful not to make any noise, was that the look on Catie's face was one he was coming to know: fear, then bravery, then determination. She bent her head to talk to the crying girl, and Jake knew that she'd seen him for what he truly was: hollow.

chapter 11

Catie thought she'd be happy for something to take her mind off of Jake. She was wrong.

Catie froze right in the middle of the bar when she realized where she'd seen the thin-faced man in the dark grey suit before. It had been bugging her all night, ever since he'd come in and settled at a table in the other server's section. Catie had counted herself supremely lucky that Danny was able to get her this gig covering shifts while he went on tour with a theater group—it meant cash to replenish her quickly dwindling savings, it meant she'd be able to actually pay Danny rent for the use of his couch, and it meant she might have more time to help her grandmother. And it meant she might be able to think about something other than Jacob Jayson for the night.

'Might' being the operative word.

The bar was the hipster version of a rowdy kind of place—so, like, ironic rowdy—but it catered to people who could afford the bottle service, or were beautiful enough that it didn't matter. Not necessarily her favorite sort of haunt, but hell, she could cocktail anywhere, and they were in need. She'd quickly been able to tell that the man in the dark grey suit wasn't there socially. He was working, just as much as she was, and it showed on his face right up until the moment his clients—she assumed they were clients, or maybe potential clients—walked in. The clients looked like a scruffy band out of Brooklyn, on the cusp of hitting it big. Catie had figured the man in the suit was an agent or a manager, maybe in public relations. She'd seen it a million times before in L.A.

And it had hit her: she'd actually seen the *same guy* in L.A. He must do pretty well for himself, agenting or managing or public relations-ing. She'd made a mental note to let the other waitress know, and then she'd gone about doing her job.

Right up until she realized that wasn't the only place she had seen him. She'd seen him at Volare, too. And she hadn't seen him in a bar in Los Angeles. She'd seen him in Brazzer's office.

That was when the world stopped.

A big guy with a neck beard jostled her and tried to apologize in an affected southern twang that he probably thought was flirtatious. Catie blushed, first because she'd been lost in a moment of terror, and then because the physical movement reminded her of the ben-wa balls she wore inside her. It was an immediate jolt, a sudden, sexual reminder of Jake—and of what had happened, and of how vulnerable she'd just become. Belatedly, it knocked some sense into her: she couldn't very well figure this out standing stock still in the middle of the bar like she had a spotlight on her, just waiting for the man in the dark grey suit to get a good look at her.

"Taking my smoke break!" she shouted at the bartender.

"I thought you didn't smoke?"

But she was already through the swing doors that led to the back storerooms and the alley entrance.

Shit. Shit, shit, shit.

She had spent the past few days ever since she'd shown up, apparently unannounced, at Stephan's House, convincing herself that she really could go through with her original plan. She could do it. She could write the story, she could make it truthful, she could save what was left of her family. She had dealt with her anxiety about being found out, about her eventual exposure, by being realistic. Not everything could possibly be as welcoming and nurturing and wonderful as it seemed at Volare, and she felt like she'd finally seen the darker side. First, Roman had brought her into his office to announce that he would be her mentor, but he'd only done that to foist her back on Jake as soon as possible. Which, at first, she hadn't minded, but then she'd gone to Stephen's House to get background for some catalog, as instructed, and Jake had been...

He'd been different.

Well, not entirely different. She'd been thinking

about it all week, trying to figure it out. None of it made sense, was the problem.

Nothing she'd been able to find about Jake — about Jacob Jayson — had seemed like it fit the man that she herself had encountered. Some of it Catie remembered or already knew. His mother had been a sort of free-spirit heiress, indulging in all kinds of weird ashrams and fads, doing all kinds of drugs, lots of lovers. Had Jake out of wedlock when she was in her forties, no mention, ever, of who the father was. Anthea Jayson seemed to court the newspapers, reveling in the attention, in scandal and notoriety. And when Jake was born he apparently became a part of the show. Like a theater prop.

And then Jake himself: not too much tabloid coverage of him as soon as he got old enough to avoid it. The opposite of his mother, in that sense, which didn't surprise Catie; she knew all about trying to get away from the kind of people your parents were. There were only a few society page mentions: when his mother died while he was away at Harvard, and then when he published his book on Shakespeare. A few academic articles, but they all tapered off, like he'd stopped taking his academic career all that seriously. And then a few mentions in the gossip rags, and then, five years ago, everything just…stopped.

It was like he'd disappeared. Like he'd just rejected public life, and instead threw himself into…Volare.

Catie realized she really had developed certain expectations about Jake, and maybe that hadn't been entirely fair. She'd watched him, obviously, when he tended bar at Volare—tended bar! The heir to the Jayson fortune! His family built the freaking *railroads*, and who knows what else—and he was always so...solicitous. Like making sure everyone was ok, and everything functioned well, was his job. And then when he'd caught her, he'd been so high-minded about it. Noble, actually. 'Noble' was the word she was looking for. Determined to do right by everyone, and with the integrity to go talk to Roman, but still keep his promise to her. He'd gone from being the impossibly hot but remote Dom that she fantasized about to this impossibly hot Dom who was also impossibly chivalrous—who she still fantasized about. Who wouldn't love that?

But now that she thought about it, she never could recall Jake in any kind of intimate conversations. The Volare lounge was this unspoken safe place for the kinds of people who frequented the club, the kinds of people who were often isolated by their own power, or fame, or wealth. It wasn't unusual for people to come there for comfort, and Jake would watch over them. He would keep an eye on everyone, but he was never the one anyone cried to. He never involved himself personally whenever anyone had a problem. He made sure someone else did that. Catie herself had done more of that, just hanging around the lounge and talking to people, the way she did.

And then there was what had happened at Stephan's House.

Catie kicked open the delivery door that opened on a side alley and propped it open with a brick. She didn't actually want to go outside—January in

New York *sucked;* she did not understand why anyone who could live in California would choose to deal with this suckage instead—but she needed the fresh air. Thinking about Jake always clouded her mind.

She wondered, for the millionth time, whether she'd made too big a deal about what had happened. What *had* happened, really? She'd walked into the bathroom and the sounds of crying behind one of the stalls had transported her immediately back to high school, when half the girls she knew had had serious problems, and she felt like she'd known exactly what to do. The girl's name had been Alice. Alice had half-heartedly cut at herself, and was almost as upset about falling back into bad patterns like that as she was about what had made her cry. She'd said that—"bad patterns"—and Catie could tell Alice had been to therapy—therapy most likely provided by Jake and Stephan's House.

Alice had just talked. Man, that kid had been through more stuff...

And Catie had just listened, tried to let the girl know she cared. When the door had opened and Jake had walked in, Catie had had this momentary thought of the two of them, together, helping Alice. Like playing house. She'd wanted very badly to see Jake help Alice. He'd been a jerk to Catie all day, but in a way, that was so inept it was almost funny, and if it had been a movie, this was where Jake would have shown his true colors, saved the day, been the hero. He'd be someone Alice could rely on.

Instead he'd gotten this *look*. And then he'd

walked away.

The look itself had been weird. Odd. Like this flash of raw emotion—of *pain*, almost—and then, like a curtain had been a drawn across his face, it was gone, and all that had been left was...nothing. His face had become a blank. And he walked away. He'd seen there was someone in trouble, he'd felt *something*, and then he had walked away.

Suddenly, Jacob Jayson didn't seem like someone anyone should rely on.

Maybe that was a bit harsh. Obviously Catie's reaction to that would be more personal. She had kind of a grudge against people who left other people hanging. She'd tried to figure out what Stephan's House was all about—narcissism? Control? An attempt to clean up the family name after years of his mother's exploits? Maybe just the best he could do, even with all that money? No, that wasn't fair. Obviously, the truth had to be more complicated. She knew she was being irrationally judgmental, but she wasn't having a rational reaction. She was having an emotional one. She just couldn't understand walking away from someone who was in pain. But Jake did, and it meant he was like all the other people who had disappointed her in life. He was no better. Maybe not worse, but no better. It meant she had been living a fantasy these past few months at Volare.

And all that made her think maybe she could go through with Brazzer's exposé after all. Except now there was a man outside, in the bar, who had seen her at Brazzer's office, and who had seen her at Volare. A *member* of Volare. Obviously, the man in the dark grey suit hadn't recognized her; she doubted he remembered every young actress type he saw in L.A., even the ones who showed up in a tabloid office. The man in the grey suit must have been there placing a story or making a deal for one of his clients to get photographed "candidly" by the paparazzi—stuff like that happened all the time. He probably hadn't even noticed her.

Right?

"Shit," she said to the empty alley.

The real, if remote, possibility that she might be exposed, in the very way she was planning on exposing Volare—well, no, she would do a better job, she'd make it look good, otherwise she couldn't live with herself—made it all very real. And there was the fact that it was Friday, and she'd decided to obey Jake's order, even though she had to cover a shift, even after all that. She had, as he'd instructed, carefully inserted the ben-wa balls, thinking of him the whole time. Why? What was wrong with her? Even now, she could feel them inside her. They kept her...not constantly aroused, unless she thought about Jake. But constantly aware.

That's what pissed her off, if she were being honest. What made it a challenge, still, to commit to what she had to do. She was disappointed in Jake, and she was hurt by that disappointment, hurt in a way that felt bigger than just one man, like she'd had a glimmer of hope that maybe some people, somewhere, wouldn't let you down, and she'd pinned those hopes, fairly or unfairly, on Jake. And yet still, *still*, thinking about him could get her hot. He still had a hold over her. She still dreamed about him, about the things he'd already done to her. He was still inside her head, and now…

Catie shuddered. She could psychoanalyze herself later. Right now she had to figure out what the hell she was going to do about the potential disaster waiting for her out in the bar. She had to get her story straight in case he recognized her from Volare, and she had to come up with something in case he recognized her from Brazzer's. That was the real danger. She'd go dye her hair or something tomorrow, but right now she had to wing it. She pulled her hair back and rolled it into a makeshift pile, sticking a pencil through it. That would have to do for now, and she'd known some men to be fooled by less than an updo.

She took a deep breath, promised herself she wouldn't think about Jake, and forced herself through the double swing doors.

And walked right into Jacob Jayson.

chapter 12

Another physical shock; another jolt that rattled the ben-wa balls. Only this time, it was the man himself standing in front of her. Catie's throat suddenly felt very dry.

"We need to talk," Jake said.

She shook her head. This was nuts. "How did you even find me?"

He seemed annoyed at the digression. "Your emergency contact on your Volare application, one Daniel Boylan, was very forthcoming, if difficult to understand while on a bus full of actors. We need to talk," he said again.

"Not now we don't," she said. She could see the man in the grey suit over Jake's shoulder. If he saw her with Jake, he'd recognize her for sure—and he'd be one step closer to connecting the dots between her, Volare, and Brazzer.

Jake's eyes flashed.

"You remember our agreement?"

"It wasn't a contract."

"It's not a contract in any legally binding sense. It is in a morally binding sense. Training does not work without a full commitment. I *have* committed. I allowed you to—" Jake broke off, as though genuinely aggravated. Catie watched him roll his neck, like a fighter between rounds, and had two thoughts: *Holy crap, that is sexy*, and, *I can't believe I have the power to get under Jacob Jayson's skin.*

"Training is not a part time endeavor," he said, looking down at her. "And while I am your trainer, *you are my sub.*"

A shiver went through her. She tried to hide her smile, shifted her weight, and was reminded— again—of the ben-wa balls. This time, it felt like her whole body quivered. She finally met his eyes, and thought she saw something searching, something questioning. Did he think she would back out?

The hope she'd felt in him flickered back to life, and with it, her conflict over what she had to do for Brazzer. She quickly squashed both thoughts; she was so tired of *thinking*. And here, in front of her, was this man who made her happy to feel instead.

"I'm working, *sir*," she said, carefully emphasizing the word. "I just took a break. I can't leave Giselle on the floor by herself, unless—"

"Who is Giselle?" he said.

"The other waitress."

"Wait here."

Catie watched Jake stalk off into the crowd, his expensive suit completely out of place amongst the carefully hip crowd. He wasn't dressed like the man with the grey suit—Jake was more Saville Row than Fifth Avenue—but he was still in a suit, and that was probably enough. Sooner or later, the man with the grey suit would notice him, would recognize him, and if he saw him with Catie…

She tried to fade into the background, hugging the double doors. She could still see the man in the grey suit through the crowd, his head swiveling around. Probably looking for his waitress. Catie turned her back, doing her best to huddle in the corner.

Suddenly she felt him behind her. Jake. His hand on her shoulder, on her waist, turning her to face him. Her body reacted almost violently where he touched her, like it was a near burn. He blocked out everything. Just the mass of him, of his tall, athletic, patrician body, like some kind of Greek statue—he seemed somehow denser then everything around him, more solid. All she could hear, see, and touch was him.

"Giselle says to take as long as you like," Jake said. "She also says thank you."

"For what? What did you—"

He leaned in, stopping just short of touching her, his lips a hair's breadth away from hers. She could feel the heat coming off his body. Could hear the rumble in his throat. He said, "Does it matter?"

She caught her breath.

"No," she whispered.

How could she already be so useless? Such a pile of hormones? Two minutes ago she'd been condemning this man, and now she would probably run away with him to Morocco if he asked.

Jake pushed her back through the double doors, and then they were in the wide hall, lit by bare, ugly fluorescent bulbs, the door to the alley on one end, the door to the storage rooms on the other.

"What did you want—?"

He cut her off. "Somewhere more private," he said.

"There's just the storage rooms," she said doubtfully, looking down the hall.

Without waiting he grabbed her hand and led her down the hall, walking almost too fast for her to keep up. She was wearing comfortable shoes—you had to, to run drinks in a bar like this—but her skirt was short and her shirt low cut, and practically running in the colder air of the hall with the ben-wa balls inside her made her feel very…alive. Jake pushed open the storage room door and pulled her inside.

It was even colder in here, and dark. The cold storage was on the other side of the room, but the whole place was cold. Unheated. Catie could see her breath in the cool fluorescent light that streamed in from the window on the storage room door.

"Is everything ok?" she asked.

"I need you to listen," he said. "This will be difficult for me to say."

Catie could only see one half of his face in the light, but it was enough to recognize the signs of struggle, as though he were physically wrestling the words out from some part of his mind that very much wanted to keep them hidden. She had followed him here, overwhelmed by her physical desire for him, in spite of what she'd thought of the man after watching him walk out on that girl; now she was held in place by her desire to see that man come forward and speak.

"You should not have been at Stephan's House," he finally said. "Roman sent you… I do not know why Roman sent you. But he surely knew it would result in something like what happened."

"What did happen?" she asked quietly.

"What happened was that you saw a man who knows his own limitations and respects them. Normally I would not feel the need to explain myself, but our situation is…unique."

"Our situation?"

Somehow she felt, right then, with certainty, that he wanted to touch her. And she wanted him to. But they both remained still, just a few inches of chilled air between them.

"Your notes," he finally said. "Your thesis. Our arrangement."

Catie tried to tell herself she wasn't disappointed. Of course that's what he meant. Of course it was.

But she couldn't quite keep it out of her voice.

"I still don't understand what you mean," she said. "About…your limitations."

"Don't lie," he said sharply. "I *saw* you. I saw you look at me, when I interrupted you and Alice. *I saw that you saw.*"

She thought back, thought back to the expression that had been on his face: pain, and then emptiness. But first, pain.

"You don't know what I saw," she said, her natural stubbornness taking over. She poked him in the chest. "*I* don't know what I saw, either, but I damn well have a better idea than you do. Why did you leave like that? Isn't that your thing? To help those kids?"

He was silent. She poked him in the chest again.

"Well?"

This time he caught her hand. He brought it back to her side and to the small of her back. Then he drew her toward him until she was pressed into his hard, muscled leg, his face hovering right over hers.

"I told you once before that I am not built for attachments," he said, very low. "It is more than that. I am not…capable of the normal things that people do in those situations. There are reasons why, but it no longer matters what they are. It remains that I am deficient in this area, that I cannot be of aid when people…*feel*. And given Alice's state of mind, it is likely that she would interpret my deficiencies as a reflection upon her. She would take them personally. It would harm her even more. I could not allow that to happen, and so my only alternative was to leave, and make sure that someone with the right skills found her."

Catie felt her defenses crumbling, felt all her hard won rationalizations fading into paper-thin excuses. If he did what he did because he thought it was the best he could do, and not because he just didn't want to be there, didn't care…

"You're not deficient in any way that I can see. You *chose* —"

"Then you are not looking," he said sharply. "I cannot feel the way normal people do. My heart…hardens."

"Oh, bull*shit*. I *saw* you," she said. "You looked like someone had kicked you in the 'nads, and *then* you left."

There was a moment of silence, and then a slow smile spread across his face. "That's fairly accurate, actually."

"Yeah, I'm calling bullshit," Catie said.

Why are you making this harder on yourself? Let him be the bad guy!

The nearness of him was working on her, slowly, the way it takes a minute or two for a martini to hit on an empty stomach. The warmth of his body, the scent of him, the way his thumb had begun to stroke at the small of her back where he still held her hand: all of it seeping into her struggling mind, making it difficult to think. To dissemble. To be the liar she needed to be.

She could tell he was holding his breath, and a tension radiated out from him, his shoulders suddenly rigid, his brow furrowed in the dull half-light. His hand on hers pressed into the small of her back, pushing her body up against the hard length of him. His other hand moved quickly in the dark to grasp her breast, and she gasped in surprise. He squeezed, hard, his thumb digging into her nipple, and a little moan escaped her lips.

"I didn't come here just to explain myself," he said, and his hand began a slow journey down the front of her body.

"Then why—"

"I came," he said, his fingers raking down the front of her stomach, leaving chills in their wake, "to make sure that you obeyed my order."

Her whole body tensed, and the resistance of the

ben-wa balls sent another shiver through her. They'd kept her at a point of tension all day, hovering there, thinking about *him*.

"Have you come?"

"No, sir."

"It's Friday," he reminded her. His hand had reached her skirt and was dragging it up her to her waist.

"I know," she said.

He slipped his hand between her thighs and pushed right and then left, prodding them open. He stroked the sensitive skin right at the seam of her leg, toying with the edge of her underwear, and she felt her whole body bear down with a pressure that was returned by the ben-wa balls still inside her. The muscles around her core, that wrapped around deep inside her, began to throb, the tension they'd felt all day rushing to the surface.

He hooked his fingers around the fabric of her underwear and pulled it aside. Her breath hitched, and she couldn't help but move her hips ever so slightly. She thought she saw him smile again.

His fingers worked back and forth, back and forth, along the length of her folds, her wetness spilling out and covering his hand. She was suddenly wetter than she could ever remember being, and only for him.

He found the string, threaded his fingers through the hook.

"Very good," he said, and pulled on it.

A small sound escaped her, and her back arched, her chest pressing into him. The pressure was almost unbearable when he pulled, the balls stretching her entrance from the inside, the feeling of fullness overwhelming her. The tension that had built up all day threatened to spill over. Her body clamored for release in a rising chorus, and something else with it, something else she couldn't ignore: the way she felt about Jake.

Why was she arguing this point? He claimed to be a heartless robot, and that would make her job *easier*. She wouldn't have to worry about hurting him, she could just go ahead and write her story, get the money from Brazzer, and then...

But he wasn't a heartless robot. She knew that, even if he somehow didn't. She'd seen it. And if he wasn't a hollow man, then he did what he did because it was the best he thought he could do. Maybe that's what Stephan's House was: his attempt to be the best version of himself. She didn't *want* that. She wanted him to be bad; she wanted him to be easy to betray.

And he wasn't.

"Dammit," she whispered.

"Tell me," he said. His voice had grown rough, and now his fingers moved quicker. She felt him close, felt him nearly inside her again, nearly inside her head, like he could feel the conflict gathering there. Could she hope to lie?

"Maybe you're fucked up," she whispered, unable to stop herself, barely able to breathe, "But you're not heartless. I saw it. I saw you. Please don't make me say anything else."

And now that she said it, what was she going to do? It was out there, it was real; she couldn't pretend it wasn't.

What was *he* going to do?

There was a timeless beat where neither of them

moved, and then he pushed her back, still holding her between her legs until the backs of her legs hit a low shelf, and then he tilted her head back and kissed her.

He *kissed* her.

His lips were softer than they looked, his tongue gentle against hers. She hadn't ever expected to be kissed by him. It was too…personal. But his mouth covered hers, and what was gentle soon grew hungry, demanding. He'd let go of her hand, and she clawed at his suit, wishing there was nothing between them. His hands pushed her skirt up high above her waist and grabbed roughly where the backs of her thighs met her buttocks, and in another second he'd lifted her up onto the low shelf and pushed himself between her legs.

Every touch drew stronger contractions out of her, every muscle awake with the near-painful pressure of the ben-wa balls. She felt his hand between her legs again, and wrapped around the string, and she knew a moment before he did it what was going to happen.

"Oh God," she said. "I don't know if you can…"

"I need to be in you," he said. "*Now*."

He pulled, and she moaned, unable to speak, and he pulled again, with sustained tension now, and she panted into his shoulder. It almost hurt; it *did* hurt, a little, to feel them pulled up against her the tight, tense flesh.

She grabbed at his neck and groaned as he pulled them out of her, her muscles rippling in waves throughout her body. The sudden emptiness made her want him, *need* him, inside her.

"Please," she choked, but he was already out,

his cock poised, the head nestled between her folds, teasing her. She clutched at his shoulders, tried to pull him into her. "Oh God, please, just—"

He pushed her back against the cinderblock wall and pulled her bottom to the edge, angling her up to him, and then he buried himself in her. She opened her mouth, gasped, as he filled her, stretching her even further than the ben-wa balls had. The tension that had been building centered, wrapped around her holding him inside her, and she could have actually cried she needed him to move so badly. He sighed, his shoulders rounding so that she felt like she was drowning in him, like he was a wave poised above her, about to crash down.

"Come for me," he growled in her ear.

And then he crashed over her.

chapter 13

Roman Casta was not a man most people felt comfortable lecturing. Admonishing, even. It's not that they didn't ever want to, or even attempt to, it was that whenever they got underway — whenever they'd worked themselves up to it — they were inevitably met with his stare. That was enough to quell most.

Not Jacob Jayson.

"Explain," Jake said, slamming the door behind him. "Right now."

Roman looked up from his computer, seemingly unfazed. He was always unfazed. The ever-in-control Roman Casta.

"Do you want to know about the cosmos?" Roman said, smiling slightly. "The movements of the planets? The laws of nature? You are starting very broad, my friend."

"I say this as your friend, Roman," Jake said. "You are one arrogant son of a bitch."

They stared at each other.

"The problem is that you have not specified what it is you wish me to explain," Roman finally said, leaning back in his chair. "And I see at least three possibilities."

Jake made a visible effort to keep his voice calm. "I tell you I have learned something that I believe to be a risk to Volare, and that by training Catie Roberts, I may be able to eliminate it. I then tell you, as a matter of conscience, that I am concerned about my personal reaction to Catie Roberts, that it may prevent me from being effective. Or impartial. And your response to this is to send her to Stephan's House with no warning? To send her to the place that is most personal, most—"

"You agreed that Stephan's House would be a beneficiary of the Valentine's Auction."

"But there was no reason to involve her!"

Roman cocked his head. "There is no reason she is necessary to the Valentine's benefit, this is true, but that is not the same thing as no reason at all. I think you know that."

"I am not a puppet, Roman," Jake said. "I am not someone to be manipulated or controlled for my own good."

"I do not think of you as puppet. I think of you as a friend. And I want what is best for my friends."

"That! That's the arrogance!" Jake caught himself shouting, and had to take a moment to lower his voice. "That you think you know what is best for me. You have *no* idea what you may have done."

Jake started to pace the length of the office, looking for somewhere else to direct his pent up energy.

"Why are you here now, Jacob?" Roman asked mildly. "I sent her to you on Tuesday. It is Saturday morning. You have another session scheduled, do you not? Why wait?"

"I've made other arrangements for today."

Jake almost said, "for her training," but stopped himself at the last minute. He couldn't quite bring himself to make a final decision on that. He had meant to, but simply hadn't. Much like he couldn't quite bring himself to stay away from her the previous night, much like he couldn't keep his hands off her. She'd said he wasn't heartless. It had stayed with him, like a persistent echo that needed answering. Only he didn't know how to answer it.

"You are upset, Jacob," Roman said. "More so than you would be if you simply…encountered her there."

Jake sat down, collapsing into the chair across from Roman. It was true. He had never felt so conflicted before. The image of Catie's face as she turned to Alice, the same expression she'd had when she admitted she had no one…it gnawed at him. He'd thought on it, rolled it over in his mind, tried to see it from every angle: why had it gotten to him? And late, late last night, after he'd left Catie, after he'd failed to control himself, yet again, he'd come back, again, to bravery.

She was simply so willing to feel for others. *With* others. She hadn't blinked, not at baring herself to

Jake, not at making herself available to Alice. She had made visible the process that came so naturally to others, and yet had eluded him for years.

And all the time, he was sure she was hiding something from him.

Roman seemed to be reading his mind, as he so often did. Jake's old friend leaned across his desk, and fixed him with a knowing look.

"Tell me, Jacob. Have you made any progress on the thing you believe to be a threat?" he asked.

Jake laughed at himself. "Not to speak of, no. I have managed to neglect that horribly."

"Do I need to ask why?" Roman said gently.

Jake looked up. He had spent much of his life figuring out what and who he could trust. He found, much to his own surprise, that he trusted what he'd seen in Catie at Stephan's House. He found, again to his own surprise, that he apparently could not trust himself around Catie. And he knew there was something she wasn't telling him; he could feel it. To a normal person, that might be the most important thing—that she was keeping something from him—but to Jake, the fact that he could feel with her at all, that he could feel so close to her and not shut down, that dark and light were able to coexist at once in what he felt for her: that was practically a miracle. It was what had motivated him so far.

And it meant he could not trust himself.

Jake rose, eyed his friend steadily. "Roman, someone, someday, is going to remove that smug look from your face. My money is on Lola."

It was the first time Roman didn't have a witty retort. Jake smiled and left in search of Catie so that he might explain.

~ ~ ~

Catie smiled brightly and tried not to show her fear.

"So what do you think, Catie?" Lola said, watching Catie carefully. "Are you up to it?"

Catie was sitting in Lola's office—already, this was messing with her head; it was supremely difficult not to think about what she'd been doing the last time she was in this room—apparently being asked to do more work in preparation for the Valentine's Auction. She was being asked to write the copy for the entire catalog. She was being asked to do this by Lola, who sat in front of her, and by a man named Vincent Duran, who sat next to her.

Vincent Duran, who had been in the bar the previous night wearing a grey suit, scaring the crap out of Catie as the only man who could place her in both Volare and Brazzer's office.

Vincent sat in the chair next to hers, studying her face. Several times he'd seemed on the verge of speaking. Catie hadn't had time to dye her hair or change her appearance. She sat before him just as she had sat in Brazzer's office just a few months ago.

"I don't really know," Catie said carefully. "I'm not sure what it is you need me to do, exactly. I don't see what's so special about writing copy."

"Your mentor didn't clue you in on Valentine's Auction?" Duran asked. Catie didn't want to look at him. It felt like tempting fate.

"No."

"Just like Roman," Lola muttered. "He requested you for this, but told you nothing." She smiled at Catie, but Catie detected some of the suspicion she'd felt from Lola weeks ago when Lola had suggested she formalize her place at Volare and become an employee. It had seemed like a way of drawing her in. Catie had been grateful that Lola had never followed up on what happened to the missing employment forms. Now she wondered whether she should be concerned, instead.

"Catie, the Valentine's Auction is unique among our events in that it is, to some degree, public," Lola said, catching Vincent's eye.

Wait. That could change everything. Catie said, "Public? Like, *public* public? I thought everything was secretive, invitation only…"

"Exactly," Vincent said. "Both. It happens in public, because that shit is hot, and because — what was the old reason again?"

Lola smiled behind her hand. "It offered cover to our more prominent members in the early days of Volare, according to Roman. Now it's mostly tradition, and, of course, it's…entertaining. The members expect it. Vincent here is in public relations. His job in this case is to do the opposite of what he usually does."

"I make it look like what's supposed to look like, a charity auction, but fashionable, right? Control the perception, fill the seats with the right people, etcetera, etcetera. And you make sure the catalog says the right things to the people who know how to read it. Which is most of them." Vincent leaned all the way back on one arm of his chair, his fingers resting on his chin, as though wanting to get a better look at Catie from another angle.

"I'm sorry, what does that mean?"

"It means many of the lots to be auctioned off are exactly what you'd expect from a Volare auction," Lola said. "A night with so and so, a particular act, whatever. But they are mixed in with other, vanilla lots—the sorts of things you would expect to find at a normal auction. Paintings. Vases. Your job will be to write the catalog according to code. Members of Volare will understand it."

There was a pause.

"Seriously?" Catie said.

"I know it sounds silly, but you'd be surprised how much fun it is," Lola said, retrieving an ominous looking folder from her desk. "People look forward to it all year long. Besides, it's for charity."

Catie stared at the folder. "So what is that?"

"These are descriptions of the lots on offer, vanilla and kinky, and the codes you'll need to apply."

Catie swallowed.

Names. Biographical details. Shit they're into.

Catie could imagine Brazzer's delight. That folder represented everything he'd pay dearly for. It represented maybe a year of her Nana's care, with some left over to live on. It probably represented a job at *Sizzle*.

It made her feel sick.

"Why me?" Catie said.

There was another pause, this one just a little too long. Catie thought Lola and Vincent were trying not to look at each other.

"Roman suggested you himself," Lola finally said.

Catie smiled weakly. "Seems like pretty sensitive information. You want me to take that home?"

Vincent laughed, his pointed teeth flashing. "You're joking, right? We've got enough security problems."

"You'll have to work from here, if that's all right."

"Security problems?" Catie said, alarmed.

"Vincent's heard rumors of an impending tabloid exposé," Lola said. "He's working on it. I'm not worried."

Catie felt the weight of both sets of eyes. She hoped she was imagining it. She hoped she was only being self-conscious. Because otherwise, she had no idea what the hell was going on. Why would they ask her to do this if they suspected her? But Vincent was "working" on it. What did that mean? Was he looking for her? Looking for the other person Brazzer had said was "on it?"

What would happen if they found out? If they knew, for real, who she was and what she was doing here?

What would Jake do?

She flinched. She couldn't bear the thought. Not after what had happened last night. She still hadn't quite processed it. Still didn't know exactly how she felt about it. But she had fallen asleep thinking about Jake, and she'd woken up thinking about Jake, and the whole time she'd wondered at the fact that he went to such lengths to do his best. To reach past what he called his natural limitations. To make sure someone would be there. To make sure *she* knew that someone would be there.

And the whole time, he thought he was heartless.

"Catie?" Lola said.

"Sorry," Catie said. "Can I think about it? I'm just a little distracted. I have a session scheduled in maybe five minutes. It's...on my mind." She gave a shy little smile.

Lola's voice softened. "I was asked to include you in one of the morning's group classes instead. I don't think Jake will continue to be available."

Catie shook her head, smiling, until she saw that Lola was serious. She'd been...bumped. Without a phone call. Passed off, without explanation. First Jake had tried to scare her off by being an asshole, then he *was* an asshole, and then he made a difficult, heart-rending apology while trying to explain himself, all the time giving her the best sex of her life while insisting they not become personally attached to each other. And now this.

It shouldn't be that big a deal, should it? It should make her choice easier. Then why did she feel like she was about to cry? She should take the folder. She should take it right now, copy what she could. She should take the contents straight to Brazzer.

She didn't wait to hear what they had to say. She'd heard bad news like this too many times, in too many different ways. She thought about her father, she thought about her grandmother, she thought about the bored voice of Mr. Everett, she thought about all her shitty ex-boyfriends, and she felt a slow, steady, inexorable tide of panic rising inside her, winding its way around her gut, wrapping itself around her chest, slowly threatening to squeeze the life out of her.

"I'm sorry," she said, stumbling her way towards the door. "I have to go."

Catie ran blindly out the door and away from Volare.

chapter 14

The weather was still terrible, a freezing rain spit sideways out of an angry sky, the wind battering the pedestrians into the sides of buildings. The boutique hotel that housed Volare on its top floor was in a trendy, gentrified part of the city, which meant no subway within a sane distance. There was only an exposed bus stop, the pitiful shelter long since ripped away, ice covering the bench.

For a moment, Catie didn't mind the biting cold. It fit how she felt: angry, bitter, furious with herself for feeling guilty. For not accepting that folder. For being such a coward, for being foolish, for being unable to decide who to be, one way or the other. She'd finally had a worthwhile goal in life, something that didn't just involve her own shallow, egotistic desires, something that was actually about someone else, and she'd fucked it up. She was fucking up because she was a sap. Because she had childish notions about loyalty and honor. Because she was so easily taken in by the promise of a man who always tried to do his best. Who was there for people, in whatever way he could be. Because she saw more in him than he saw in himself, even if he didn't want her.

But he'd warned her, hadn't he? He'd warned her not to get attached. It was her own damn fault.

If she kept crying, the tears would freeze on her cheeks. She wiped her eyes with the back of her hands and looked around for somewhere to huddle against the wind, or at least somewhere to get a hold of herself. There was a shallow alley in the middle of the block, a remnant from an older city, when deliveries were made by carts or something. Double doors in the filthy ground led down to the storage area of the restaurant on the corner. The restaurant was closed, the alley empty, and she'd be able to look for the bus from there. She jogged toward it, head down against the wind.

The sudden stillness as she entered the alley left a ringing in her ears. The wind howled out on the avenue, and the rain still fell, freezing where it hit the ground. The alley was a winter oasis, warmed by the steam vents from the buildings on either side.

But it wasn't empty.

He was huddled against a vent, scrunched up. He rose up to his full height, face half hidden by a hood, and she saw that he was thin. What might be called 'wiry' if he didn't look so strung out. She couldn't tell how old he was. Younger than her, probably.

It wasn't until he moved toward her with an exaggerated nonchalance that she remembered to be afraid. She could see his eyes moving quickly, sweeping up and down the alley while he blew into his red, raw hands.

She shouldn't have stopped. She shouldn't have made eye contact.

"You got a dollar?" he said. Like they knew each other. Were old friends.

She didn't answer.

"Gimme a dollar," he said, more forcefully.

"Sorry, I'm just on my way—"

He stepped in front of her. "Give me your fucking wallet."

Catie froze. She had imagined a scene like this a million times when she'd first decided to come to New York. She'd imagined herself fighting back, smacking the guy in the face with her bag, running away. Now she had no idea what to do. She couldn't stop thinking about what came next. If she gave him her wallet, what happened after that?

"Bitch, are you deaf?"

He took another step towards her, angry, furious, his face twisted up. Like she'd insulted him, too. Like he hated her for having money, a warm coat, for being afraid of him. Catie felt out of time, unable to move, just watching him come toward her in slow motion, until she heard her name.

"Catie?"

She snapped awake, the look of recognition on her face warning the boy with the hoodie. He hesitated, just for a moment. Catie screamed,

"Jake!"

The boy in the hoodie turned, and Catie saw Jake over his shoulder, stepping into the alley. Jake, without a coat, his suit wet from the rain. Jake, his eyes resting on her, and then on the boy. Then clouding with fury.

The boy sidestepped and ducked his head down, like he was just walking through, minding his own business. Jake charged into the alley, grabbed him by the shoulders, and threw him against the wet brick with a sickening *thud*. The kid fell to the ground, scrabbled up, and tried to run. He found Jake there, grabbing him, lifting him back up, towards the wall, with all the strength of anger and fear. Jake held him, pinned and struggling, drew a fist back, and stopped.

The boy's hood had fallen back. Jake was looking at his face.

They stood there like that, Jake breathing hard, shoulders heaving, hulking, full of adrenaline and wanting to put it somewhere, the kid looking for a way out, looking smaller and skinnier by the second. Then it happened. Catie saw it on his face: the rage drained away, that look of pain, of grief, in its place, and then he looked at *her*.

"Are you hurt?"

She shook her head. "No."

The kid made a sudden move to dart away, his ratty sneakers scuffing on the wet pavement. Jake moved quickly and grabbed him by the back of the hoodie, got hold of one wrist. He held him effortlessly, and walked them both gently back to the wall.

"Easy," she heard Jake say. "Do you have a

139

weapon?"

The kid didn't answer. She saw Jake lean forward, saw him whisper something. He turned the kid around and looked at him. Jake's face was unreadable. He stood there or a moment, not doing anything, his eyes far away. Then she saw him reach into his pockets. He gave the kid some money, a card.

The kid ran.

It was just the two of them, alone, in the cold. Jake's breath made clouds in the wet air, his dark hair plastered to his forehead, his white shirt stuck to his chest.

"You're soaked," he finally said to her.

She laughed, grateful that the rain hid her tears. Catie had no idea what she was going to do next, but she knew it couldn't involve betraying the man who'd just thrown himself into danger to save her.

~ ~ ~

It wasn't until they'd settled into a frozen silence in the back of the black town car Jake had on standby that he remembered that not all was well between them. He had only found her in that alley because she'd run. She'd run because she was upset. Because his choices had upset her. Now that the rush of near-violence was fading, the temporary closeness of a close call had fallen away, and they were left with the reality of what had come before.

He'd fucked up.

He'd been rash. He'd been so rattled by his uncharacteristic displays of emotion, by his inability to control himself around her, by the unfamiliar feelings she provoked, that he'd been even more uncharacteristically rash in his reaction, and the result was that she'd been hurt. Worse, he'd tried to deny it.

But it had all been exposed when he'd seen her, threatened, in that alley. What he'd felt then terrified him. What he'd felt himself capable of. He'd wanted to destroy that boy, destroy him utterly, until the moment that his hood had fallen back.

He'd looked so much like Stephan.

Maybe not the Stephan of better times. Maybe it was just the resemblance of a junkie.

In those slow, frozen seconds, it had all flooded back. And he'd remembered the reason he'd agreed to train Catie in the first place, the reason he hadn't just sent her to Roman to deal with: his promise. For all her posturing, for all the threat she posed to Volare, she couldn't hide her loneliness. And Volare was perfect for her. If there was ever someone who needed to discover themselves, it was her, and she was the most natural sub he'd ever encountered.

No, that wasn't quite right. She felt natural with him.

And he was supposed to help her. He could imagine Roman dealing with the issue of the thesis just fine, but he felt he should be the one to be there for Catie herself. Be there, in whatever way he could. Do whatever he was able to do. He'd forgotten, somehow, and her ability to make him feel in new, unimagined ways clouded his mind, confused his purpose. The very thing that made her special to him made it harder for him to be unselfish.

It had been difficult to convince her to even accept a ride. He felt her retreating from him even now. She looked steadily out the window, into the rain, seeing nothing, yet determined not to look at him.

"Thank you," she said suddenly.

Taken completely off-guard, he grappled for a response.

"You don't have to thank me for that," he said, embarrassed. "That was just…what one does."

Too late he realized how impersonal that sounded. He saw the edges of her head tilt more towards the window, saw her face in the reflection: it was pained.

He tried again. "I meant that the alternative was unacceptable. Not…"

Shit.

"I would not have chased just anybody out in the rain." She half turned to him. He went on. "I, in fact, have never chased anybody out into the rain. I hate the goddamn rain. And I've never been in a fight. I abhor violence. I've never understood the need for it, until today."

She had started to smile, and as he finished she looked at him with sympathy.

"You might say it was personal," she said.

He sighed. "Yes."

He had thought that would make her…well, if not happy, then perhaps satisfied? At a minimum, he would have expected that admission to relieve some of her evident unhappiness. Instead it seemed to make things worse.

He was, again, as always, with this woman, completely out of his depth.

They didn't speak again until the car turned onto Cabrini Boulevard, up on the very north end of the island, and they could both see the flashing lights in front of a dilapidated apartment building. Catie leaned forward, trying to get a better look.

"Shit," she said under her breath.

"Is that your building?" he asked. There were several fire trucks, police cars. The entire block seemed sealed off.

"Yeah." Her voice was tense, brittle. It held the fragility of a life easily upended, of the fear of circumstances beyond her control. It was a tone of voice he remembered in Eileen Corrigan, years ago.

He instructed the driver to pull up slow, rolled down his own window. He recognized a police captain from a Police Benevolent Association dinner; an up and comer, a political animal, groomed for advancement. Good. He could work with that.

"Stay here," he said. "Let me see what I can do."

Jake couldn't understand the crowds at first. Rain—especially freezing rain—usually kept away any rubberneckers, but there were what looked like hundreds of people milling about, braving the weather. He got closer and it hit him: those must be the residents. He looked up; the top floors were blackened by smoke and fire.

"Captain Seenan," he called out. It took a moment for the captain to place him. When he did, you could see the gears begin to whirl in his head. The captain called out an order and walked over.

"Mr. Jayson, what can I do for you?"

The Jayson name had its advantages.

"What's going on?"

"A fire on the top floor, fire department responds, puts out the fire, and in the process discovers serious health hazards. Whole building's being evacuated."

"When will the residents be allowed back in?"

The captain looked at him. "Serious hazards. Asbestos, electrical, structural. To be frank, the place is a shithole. Shoulda been condemned years ago. I doubt any of these city departments are gonna give the ok anytime soon. In fact, heads are probably gonna roll that the building was kept in this state. Somebody was greasing the wheels, you know?"

"You're saying it's condemned?"

"Is your interest in this personal, sir?"

That word again. Jake eyed him. "Yes, you could say that. A friend of mine has been staying here."

"Well, my best advice is to find that friend someplace else to stay, sir. I don't know how the city's going to handle this, but I don't think anyone's getting back inside that building."

Jake looked back at the town car. He could just see the shape of Catie's head in the tinted windows.

"Can I ask a favor, Captain?" he said. Those were the magic words. Captain Seenan's face lit up. Doors had opened for people who had done favors for the Jayson family.

"Name it, sir."

Captain Seenan himself escorted them past the

police tape and into the condemned building. He'd conferred briefly with some colleagues in the Fire Department, inquired about what floor Catie lived on, and told them he could give them five minutes. Catie had nodded.

"I don't have that much stuff," she said. Her voice had lost the brittle quality, and now it just seemed to come from far away. It made Jake's heart ache.

The building was as described. "Shithole" might even have been generous. Jake couldn't tell if Catie was embarrassed; she seemed occupied elsewhere, thinking hard on something. He tried not to call attention to himself, but it made him irrationally angry to think of her living here.

Three flights up the stairs, the elevator having been cordoned off, and Captain Seenan waited for them while Catie rummaged for her key. She had stopped to collect mail from a line of identical mailboxes in the lobby, and now the bundle of envelopes fell from where she'd been holding it under her arm. Jake reached down to get it for her, absurdly eager to be of aid in some stupid way, but Catie snatched the letters away, eyes wide and face white.

"Sorry," he said. "I didn't mean to…"

"It's fine." She tucked the envelopes, facing towards her, back under her arm. "Sorry, I just…"

"No, don't apologize. It's private."

For a moment, he wondered whether she'd invite him inside. In the end she didn't, but she didn't protest when he followed her in, either. She was distracted, and he thought again of what a shock this must be. He didn't think she had any family in New York, didn't know if she knew anyone else. The sight of her face when she'd admitted that she had no one to call if anything went wrong kept floating about in his mind, never far from the surface of his thoughts. Jake very much doubted she had anywhere to go. He knew where he wanted her to go, but convincing her seemed, at the moment, less than a sure thing.

The apartment was well kept, clean, bright, stylish, even—whoever lived here made the most with what they had. There were lamps made out of old Bombay Gin bottles, a spectacular fish tank, many colored lights. It made Jake smile.

"I've got to call Danny," Catie said. "Shit, he's going to... I don't know what he's going to do. He's out on tour for three months."

Jake made a mental note. He'd take care of it. But that wasn't what concerned him now.

"Catie, what are you going to do?"

She avoided his gaze. "No idea."

Before he could say anything, she disappeared into a room and emerged with a duffel bag, already half-full. She moved about the small apartment with admirable efficiency, gathering belongings and clothing from improvised storage places. Mostly clothing, some books that she stuffed quickly into the bag. A notebook that she tried to hide from him.

Jake could feel their five minutes ticking away.

"Catie, I can arrange—"

"God, you're making this difficult!" she said.

She had turned away from him. Jake walked around her and gently touched her elbow. It seemed strange that she wouldn't look at him.

"What are you talking about?" he said.

"It's complicated," she said. "I just...I can't keep doing this."

"Doing what?"

She waved her hand, as though she hadn't heard him. As if she were just thinking out loud. "But it doesn't matter, right? You don't want to train me anymore, anyway."

He turned her towards him. "No. That's not true."

When she finally looked up at him, he couldn't tell if she believed him. Somewhere on the other side of the room, a phone began to ring. Catie didn't move.

"Catie, *that is not true.* I made a mistake. Many mistakes. But our arrangement is unchanged. It must be."

"Unless I leave Volare."

He wanted to shake her, shout at her. No. That couldn't be allowed to happen. He felt nauseous, but eventually his mind caught up with his gut: it wasn't just what he wanted, it was because of her notes, her thesis. There were reasons beyond the personal. Beyond what he'd promised.

The phone continued to ring.

"No," he choked.

"Listen, you've been really kind to me today, but—"

"Come stay with me."

The words were out of his mouth before he knew what they were. His mind, his rational, controlled mind, turned them over, double-checked their meaning. No, he'd said it. He'd meant it. He wanted her with him. And he could find many

147

ways to rationalize it—that it would be easier to train (a lie), that it would be easier to keep an eye on her (and he'd be more vulnerable), that it wouldn't compromise his judgment (a vicious lie)—but the truth was, he simply wanted her with him.

Catie looked at him with disbelief. There was almost a glimmer of happiness in her face, almost relief, and then it was gone, replaced by that look of loss again. She looked at him sadly, eyes wide, head shaking, as the phone continued to ring.

Then the answering machine clicked on.

"I have an urgent message regarding the care of one Elizabeth Reardon at Ridge Hill Living Facility. There has been a change in her status, and she's been moved to the Constant Care facility, but I see on the records that her bill has only been paid for Assisted Living through the end of the Q2. Her account is only covered for Constant Care through the end of February. I was given this number by our usual contact, a Mr. Everett. Please call us back as soon as possible."

Catie turned her head toward the sound. Jake watched her face go slack as the message played, watched her eyes cloud over.

"Shit," she said softly.

"Sounds like an important message," he said, not knowing what else to say.

"It is."

They stood, silently. He fought off the interruption; she wasn't Elizabeth Reardon, this wasn't her apartment.

"Catie," he said, not wanting to let the issue die. He could feel her pulling further away from him, and he couldn't let that happen. He could fix this—he knew he could. "Catie. Come stay with me. Please."

"Oh, *shit*," she said, turning away from him. Her hand went to her face, like she was wiping her eyes.

It wasn't exactly the response he expected.

"Catie, if you want, you don't have to see me. It's a big house. You don't have to train with me—"

He stopped suddenly, stumbling over his own unexpected reaction. He felt sick. In truth, the idea of her training with anyone else was physically repugnant to him.

Jake was speechless.

"Hey, Mr. Jayson?" Captain Seenan opened the door, looked at Jake and Catie's obviously emotional tableau, and cleared his throat. "Mr. Jayson, I'm sorry, but we really only have five minutes."

Jake didn't know whether he wanted to hug or hit the captain. "Thank you, Captain. We'll be right out."

Seenan opened his mouth, thought better of it, and ducked back out.

They had a minute, maybe less. Jake stared helplessly at Catie's back, totally unsure of what to do. This was the exact space in which he was without skills, without experience: relationships. Connecting. Emoting. He knew what to do as a Dom. He would know what to do if she agreed to continue training. As a man, he was at a loss.

Time to try something.

He reached out, grabbed Catie by the arm, and pulled her back to him, spinning her around until she was pinned against his chest. He brushed aside her hair and kissed her, hard, and kept kissing her, his hands roaming over her body as he felt her begin to respond. When he pulled away, it felt like they had stepped into a scene.

"Come with me," he ordered.

"Yes," she said.

He should be elated. He was. He could feel the heat between them, knew that was still intact.

Then why did she seem so sad?

chapter 15

Catie's expression was calm while her mind rioted.

There was no other way to describe it, really. She was in a kind of shock now, so much so that she let Jake carry her duffel back down the rickety, filthy stairs, back through the rain, back to the black town car. She watched him throw it in the trunk, let him open the door for her.

Jake. Jake who'd just kissed her until her mind went blank and her body went live. Jake, who she'd thought she'd finally decided she couldn't betray; Jake, who had almost made it easy to make that choice by running after her, by putting his body between hers and danger. She'd thought she'd have at least six months to figure out something else. She'd thought she'd be able to do it; somehow, she'd make it all work out. Nana and

Jake both could rely on her, even if neither of them knew it.

Then that message.

She really didn't have a choice. She had to get that story, she had to get it written, and she had to get it to Brazzer by the end of February, or her grandmother...

Her mind clamped down. No. Nope. Wasn't going to happen. Catie did her best to steel herself for what she would have to do, but every time she looked at Jake—every time she thought about that last kiss, about the kiss before that, about every time he'd touched her—it felt like her whole body went into rebellion. How did other people live with this kind of conflict? With these lies? How did people find the strength to do the things that had to be done?

She so wished that he could be a bastard. Truly a bastard. She had thought, briefly, when he'd blown her off, that he was, and she'd been sad, at the time. Hurt. Now, she *longed* for that. She'd had no idea how lucky she'd been.

Instead, he'd become the white knight she would have to stab in the back. Maybe some part of her had known, some part of her had hedged, as she was packing her bag: she'd remembered her notebook, after all. The one with all her notes and observations in it. The one with all of Volare's secrets.

Part of her wished he would find her notebook. Part of her wished she would be exposed, and thus absolved of all responsibility for making a choice. Then she could tell herself she wouldn't have done it, in the end, that something else would have come along, that she would have figured out another way to raise the money. But she didn't really believe in fairytales like that. She knew no one would be there to save her and her grandmother in the end. It was just up to her.

So she'd have to toughen up.

"Are you all right?" Jake asked her.

She forced herself to look at him, which did *not* help. He looked incredible, his silver streak tussled where she'd had her hand in his hair, his white shirt still wet and plastered to his chest. Catie swallowed, tried to quell the feeling in her stomach. "Yeah," she said. "I'm just…I guess just…not really sure what to think of all this."

She looked ahead, wondered if the driver was listening in. Somehow that made it worse. Jake seemed to understand her concern. He nodded, and they rode the rest of the way in silence.

Catie was surprised when they pulled up to a stone-faced mansion, complete with wrought iron works and juliet balconies. She'd been admiring all the stately buildings, never imagining that one of them was Jake's actual home. Of course it made total sense, when she actually thought about it. His great-great-grandfather had probably commissioned the damn thing, back before there were even sidewalks this far north. She'd never get her head around that: his family had helped build the city. The *country*. Railroads, mining, banks…

And he was carrying her duffel bag.

He stood by the open door, bag slung over his shoulder, and held out his hand. She sighed.

Be less perfect right now. Please.

But she took it. She could feel his touch

everywhere, all over again. She held her breath, and followed him up the steps, willing herself to just get through this.

What the hell had she been thinking?

He punched a code into a number pad, then placed his thumb on a sensor, and the door clicked open. The security shouldn't have surprised her either, but it did. It also reminded her what she was there for. *She* was what he needed to secure himself against.

"Catie!"

She had faltered, stepping over the threshold. A Freudian slip, a gesture of panic, maybe. She felt exposed, and weak, and frightened that she'd never be strong enough to pull this off.

But it was worse when he caught her. His arm pressed into her where he held her around the waist, and the steel-like steadiness of the man himself as he kept her from falling made her feel even weaker. Just the nearness of him was enough to overpower her senses. Her breath hitched, and her muscles tensed, and it felt as thought her whole body seized with her desire for him. For one long, painful second, it was all she could feel.

Without a word, he threw her bag in through the door onto a staid marble floor and dipped to lift her in his arms.

"Oh Jesus," she said.

"What?"

"Nothing."

He carried her—*carried* her—in through the imposing front entrance, and slammed the door shut behind them.

It echoed.

Catie finally looked up. It was dark, but windows that seemed twenty feet high let in some streams of grey light. It was a massive entrance hall, the kind of thing you expected to read about in Edith Wharton novels, the sort of space meant to impress guests at formal events.

"You live here alone?" she asked.

"It does get a little drafty," he said, smiling in the gloom.

He walked over to where he'd chucked her bag, and set her down gingerly on the floor. She was both relieved and saddened; not feeling the warmth of him left her colder than she'd been before. Without thinking about it she let her hand drift down his arm, and only remembered herself when his eyes followed the trail of her touch.

They hadn't yet said what they were, if anything at all. Whether he was her trainer, or… It would be so much worse if this were truly personal now. Worse, but she longed for it. She wanted him to say, "I can't train you because I want you, because I care about you, because I am attached to you," and yet she dreaded it above all else. *Talk about fairytales*. As though she would be the one to change him, to make him whole. And then to betray him.

"Sorry," she said. "I didn't… I don't…"

"Follow me," he said. His voice was gentle, yet commanding. It was exactly what she needed to hear. Every time she tried to think, she was met with the terrible facts of her situation, with the awful choice she'd made. Her overheated mind was quickly becoming a battle zone.

He led her up the stairs to the second floor,

where there were soft lights, and warm looking rugs laid out over the cold stone floors. The floors above them were dark; she wondered if he ever went up there. One floor of this building looked big enough for two, maybe three normal sized apartments. Did he really live here all alone?

"I have a cook who comes regularly," he said, like he was reading her mind. That, or she wasn't the first person to wander through this lonely house thinking like this. "And regular employees, but no live-in servants. We're alone."

Alone.

Two kinky-minded people could get up to all sorts of things by themselves in a house like this. She found herself wondering if he had a special room for BDSM play, then found herself jealously wondering about who else might have played with him. It was exactly the wrong sort of thing to think, the kind of thing that would only trick her into unrealistic expectations, into caring more about him than she could afford to. As if her mind were actively trying to betray her while she was planning to betray him.

Fantastic.

He led her to the back of the house and opened a heavy wooden door to reveal an enormous bedroom. Everything about it was huge: the multi-paned windows, the bed, the drapes. It wasn't stuffy, either.

"I have the cleaning service keep it ready," he said.

"That doesn't sound like something a man who's planning on being unattached would do," she said offhand.

The immediate silence felt thick, impenetrable. Catie couldn't believe she'd said that out loud. What the hell was wrong with her? It was like she couldn't handle all of the intensity, and her circuits were blowing left and right.

"I have a large extended family," Jake finally said, smiling wryly as he deposited her bag by the side of the bed. "Sometimes they threaten to visit. I keep everything prepared almost like a good luck charm, to keep them away. So far, it's worked flawlessly."

She smiled weakly. She didn't know what she wanted — or rather, what she wanted *most* — but the sight of him, standing there, still in his wet shirt, his hair still unruly and damp, looking at her with those molten eyes, was enough to make her feel a little crazy. She was being pulled so severely in so many directions that she was sure she must be vibrating under the tension.

"Catie," he said. "I have to show you something."

She shook her head, unwilling to speak. She couldn't. She had no idea what she'd say or do. She was petrified of whatever came next.

Jake came close, and took her hands. "Please," he said.

She was a goner.

chapter 16

Jake only led her up one floor, not bothering to turn on the lights, into a wood-paneled room that looked as though it could have belonged on an English country estate. Well, except for the projection screen pulled down across one wall. And the theater-quality projector in the middle of the room.

"I feel as though I owe you an explanation," he said, walking to a shelf beyond the projector. "Well, a further explanation. Do you see these?"

Catie was just grateful to have something else to look at besides Jake. She stepped close and peered at the shelves. They were clunky canisters holding old-fashioned reels of film, with titles hand-written down the sides. Titles like, "The Seven Year Itch," "Casablanca," "The Big Sleep."

"Those are great movies," she said.

Jake's face lit up. "You've seen them?"

"Some of them, yeah. Hey, 'Sweet Smell of Success!'"

It was one of her favorite movies. Burt Lancaster as the most evil gossip columnist alive, using his power to ruin and corrupt everyone around him, all in pursuit of some twisted thing involving his sister.

"One of the best," he said. "Sex, gossip, drugs, betrayal."

That last word pierced her. "But there's a happy ending," she said.

"Not for Tony Harris," Jake smiled a little sadly.

Catie turned stiffly back to the shelf, not wanting to look at Jake. No, Tony Harris didn't have a happy ending in that film, not after he double-crossed everyone he met in the pursuit of success. He didn't deserve a happy ending. *Neither do I.*

She pulled the canister off the shelf, only to catch sight of green leather where she'd expected to see wood paneling. She reached up to gather more of the canisters, expose the small leather box that seemed hidden there, when Jake grabbed her wrist.

His touch hit her like a live wire. She froze.

"So what's so important?" she finally said. If she couldn't handle just this conversation, if she couldn't handle it any time he touched her...

"None of these are the originals," he said, touching each canister one by one. "I've had to replace them all over the years. I wore them out."

"You wore them out? You can do that?"

"Apparently. Incredibly difficult to replace,

some of these."

"So you're a movie buff," she said. This was good. Anything that got them talking about trivial, impersonal things was good. Or better, anyway.

"Not exactly," he said, turning to face her. "Not by choice, necessarily."

Catie scrunched up her face. "You were forced…?"

"No."

"Good, because I was thinking, like, 'A Clockwork Orange'…?"

He laughed. "I can't believe you know film."

"I watched a lot of television as a kid."

"When you weren't reading about Roman generals?"

She flinched. "I still can't believe I told you about that. It's actually not the greatest memory for me, you know? Kind of makes me seem pathetic and weird. Something I did to get close to my dad, and it turned out it was all a lie."

He touched her face, and she lost her voice. The short distance between them seemed too large, unnatural, begging to be filled.

"I think we have more in common than either of us first thought," he said.

She shook her head, not trusting herself to speak again. She wanted to scream, *no, don't bring us closer, I can't handle this*, but she found herself unable to stop it, unable to pull away.

"These films were given to me when I was boy," he said, his fingers brushing against her cheek. "I don't even remember who gave them to me. But when my mother had guests, which was more frequently than not, she would lock me in here. I watched these films, over and over again. I was only allowed out when she needed me for something—to parade me around, usually, take a photograph. She'd be this utterly...*affectionate* creature, in front of whomever, and then I'd be locked away again, until everyone left. Sometimes they wouldn't leave for a long time. Sometimes days. I know most of these films by heart."

"That's horrible," she whispered. "Days?"

He smiled. "There are much worse things."

"But—"

"No, Catie, there really are. There are better men than me who've come through much worse with fewer wounds. But I am what I am, and I want to explain, so that you know not to take it—"

"Personally."

He smiled again. How could he smile while talking about this? Is this why he seemed so remote? "Yes. Personally. Those were the only times she'd show me real affection, or, truthfully, seem to remember me at all. I tried to spend as much time with my father's family as I could, but, for various reasons, I wasn't always welcome. It was complicated. The results are that I am sort of...hollow. I recoil at affection. At intimacy. I cannot become attached in the way people normally do; I've tried, it fails miserably. So I don't make those promises any longer. I can't stand to disappoint people. I can't stand to hurt them, as I inevitably do. I have made that mistake before, with terrible consequences."

For the first time that she could remember, he looked down at the floor, his brows coming together in a brief expression of grief, as though remembering something he didn't want her to see.

She didn't know what to say. No, she didn't know *which* thing to say—some small part of her was saying she should be happy to be let off the hook, that he was telling her he could never feel, never trust, never care what the hell she did. But she knew, *knew*, it was a lie. She'd seen him feel for others. He was brushing her cheek with utmost tenderness right now.

"I couldn't stand to hurt you," he said softly.

"Bullshit!"

He blinked.

"I'm calling bullshit again," she said. "What are you doing right now? You're being affectionate, you're—"

"No," he said, and he threaded his hands through her hair and tightened his grip. "I just can't help but want you whenever I look at you."

Everything stopped.

Then a rush passed through Catie's body, flooded into every last corner, every crevice, every nerve. Her pulse pounded out a steady, rising beat, and she was afraid to move, afraid to breathe, unsure of what she'd do.

"That is part of what domination and submission means to me, Catie," Jake said, his hand now moving down the length of her neck. She craned toward him helplessly, unable to stop her body from responding.

"It's the way I can be close to people, through that ritual, those rules and roles. It's hard to explain. It's the way I can bring them and myself happiness. And it just…"

"It just *is*," she finished for him. Her eyelids felt

heavy, and she could feel her will weakening. But it was more than that. Something about what he'd said made sense to her on a deeper level. She thought about her own history, about her own past fighting through relationships that didn't make sense, about holding on to people who were wrong for her, and pushing away people who were kind. She thought about how her mind relaxed into scenes with Jake. How those scenes had made her feel finally...free. Like the rules and the strictures made it safe to be herself.

It was the only time she felt totally sure of who she was.

"I don't know whether it's wise for you to continue training with me," Jake said. "For your own sake."

Catie's eyes flew open. He was looking at her intently, with that same intense level of concentration he had whenever they'd...she wasn't sure what they'd done. Had sex. Made love. But that look pushed her beyond rational thought, beyond all of her anxieties and worries about what the hell she was doing there, and before she knew it, she was speaking.

"I need it," she said, and his hand stiffened on her neck. "You don't understand. It's like that for me, too, when you're...when you dominate me."

She remembered back to the first time they'd had sex, when he'd been overcome — when they'd both been overcome — in Lola's office. How her body had been wracked by him, while inside she'd felt somehow peaceful for the first time in ages. She needed that now more than ever. She needed to lose herself in subspace, needed to lose herself in him the only way she knew how.

Catie looked Jake in the eye. Then she fell to her knees, kneeling before him the way he'd ordered her to at Volare.

"Please," she said, her voice cracked. She suddenly couldn't see a way to get through this without him. Without this. She couldn't tell him why she needed it, but she did. "I need this, more than I can say. I need you to be... *Please.*"

She looked up to find him looking down at her with those fiery eyes, his jaw set hard. Something in him shifted, something darkened. His chest rose, his shoulders broadened, and she felt his fingers on the back of her head.

"Show me," he ordered.

She knew exactly what he meant. Just being on her knees in front of him in the submissive pose turned her on. But now, knowing what he wanted her to do — what he'd ordered her to do — she felt her nipples harden. She was wet already.

She reached up, slowly, and unzipped his fly. She didn't know why she should be so nervous, but she was. Tentatively, she freed his cock, feeling the weight of it in her hand. And then she just stared at it. She hadn't had much opportunity to study it in any of their earlier encounters, and now she wondered how she'd taken something so intimidating. It was bigger than she thought, fuller. She could feel his eyes on her and as she let her fingers trail down its length she felt herself slip, ever so slowly, into that freedom she felt in submitting to him.

She raised it to her lips and kissed the head.

His fingers fanned out through her hair, and

then his grip tightened. He held on, and she loved knowing that he held her there at his will. She leaned forward to draw him into her mouth and was rewarded with a rumbling groan from somewhere deep within his chest. She sucked gently on the head, moving her fingers down the shaft, wanting to feel him swell in her mouth. His hands tensed, pulling on her hair. It should have hurt. It *did* hurt, and she wanted him to do it again.

She circled the base of his cock with her hand and pushed herself forward until she felt his swollen head bump against her throat. She couldn't breathe, and she felt her eyes begin to water. She'd been overwhelmed by him in any number of ways already, but this was new. She wanted even more. She wanted him to come hot and hard in her mouth, wanted to know she'd made him lose control. She felt both powerless, her head held in his hand, and powerful, all at the same time. The need to please him had driven every other thought away.

She laved her tongue along the underside of his shaft and took him in her mouth again, faster and deeper than before, and as her hand found a rhythm with her mouth, Jake began to thrust, driving his cock to the back of her throat. She moaned, her clit throbbing, and she could tell he was about to come. She was nearly there when he yanked her head back and away from him.

His cock was huge and hard, wet with her saliva, a dark, red, angry color. She looked up at him, begging, wanting to finish him, not understanding. But he didn't even give her a chance to speak.

"Get up," he said, his voice choked and tight, and pushed her across the room, right up to the back of the leather couch in front of the screen.

They stared at each other for a moment, taking each other in. He loomed over her, dark and brooding, flexing his fists, breathing hard. His eyes trailed down her body, back up to her eyes, hungry. Catie knew what she wanted. She wanted him rough, she wanted him to push out every other thought. She needed the relief. And she wanted — needed — to know he couldn't resist her. That when push came to shove, that even when his judgment told him otherwise, he would always choose her.

For a moment, she thought he wouldn't. For a moment, she felt sorry that she had asked that of him, as unfair as it was for her to ask *anything* of him, given what she was already planning to take.

Then he raised one hand, and, with a twirl of his finger, made it very clear exactly what he wanted.

Catie opened her eyes wide and bit her lip. She couldn't resist one last look at his cock, even harder and darker now. Then she slowly turned around, her waist up against the back of the red leather couch.

And waited.

She felt his breath on her neck first, and her own breath quickened in anticipation. It seemed ages before he moved, before he touched her, and she was already feeling lightheaded by the time she felt his hand under her skirt. He ran his hand along the seam of her underwear, and followed it down until he reached his fingers between her legs. She sighed as he stroked her, the contact both pleasurable and almost painful, she was so swollen. The fabric clung to her wetness where he gripped her, and she was sure she could come just like that if he stroked her long enough.

But then his hand was on her neck, on the muscle sliding down to her shoulder. He squeezed, and then quickly pushed her down, roughly bending her over the back of the couch. She made a sound, shortened by the pressure of the couch on her stomach, and bit her lip again, afraid that if she said anything, he'd stop. She wanted him so badly she could barely breathe.

He pressed his leg between hers, spreading them. He took whatever time he wanted. He could surely tell how badly she wanted him, how badly she needed him inside her, and still, he took his time. She was on the verge of begging.

He pushed her skirt up above her waist, and her underwear bit into her hips as he twisted them in his fist, pulling them aside. Her legs were trembling, and she arched her back into him as he bent her even lower.

Her pulse roared in her ears. She felt completely vulnerable. At his mercy.

There was no more preamble, no warning. The head of his cock touched her outer lips, and then it pushed into her, slowly but relentlessly, so that she felt each thick inch. It kept coming, the slow, deliberate motion of his thrust giving her time to wonder how he'd fit. She moaned as he slowly impaled her, dropping her hands to the seat of the couch to push herself back against him. She felt stretched, full, on fire.

Then he started to fuck her.

He dropped his hand to the small of her back,

not letting her up, and his fingers dug into her hip as he drove in and out in long, strong, punishing thrusts. She stopped trying to buck her hips back at him and gripped at the leather of the couch, holding on, while he picked up the tempo.

"Come for me," he growled.

She heard herself gurgle something unintelligible and then just stopped trying to speak at all and rode the feeling that was coming over her. Her body both opened and closed at the same time, trying to draw him in, contracting around him, and finally bursting in great shuddering waves that flew down her trembling legs.

She'd come hard, but not enough, and he wasn't done. When her legs wouldn't hold her anymore he pushed her forward on the back of the couch, balancing her there, and kept going, slowing the pace until she started to build with him again, until she was screaming something, not words. He drove into her with one, final thrust and she felt him come hot and hard, felt him shudder against her, and then fall, the exhausted weight of him laying on top of her, leaving them both motionless.

It felt like a long time before he lifted himself off of her. She might have stayed on the couch like that, limp and exhausted, if he hadn't wrapped his arm around her waist and pulled her up. He brought them both over to the couch and pulled her down on his lap. They sat like that, still and quiet, for a long time.

Finally, he said, "I have a collar for you."

chapter 17

"What the hell's the matter with you?"

Eileen's voice pierced Jake's foggy mind and dragged him back to reality. Her characteristic perceptiveness, delivered in her equally characteristic style — bluntly — put him on edge. For days, ever since Catie had come to stay with him, he'd been a useless, preoccupied mess. He was having enough trouble sorting through his own emotions, let alone Catie's, and he didn't think he was in the mood to have Eileen shine a harsh light on whatever uncomfortable truths lay at the root of his trouble.

Not that he had a choice.

"Seriously, Jakey, what's the deal? You look terrible."

Eileen rummaged through her beige leather bag,

her green eyes narrowed and locked on his face. He hadn't even noticed her cab pull up, though he'd arrived a few minutes early just to give himself a chance to prepare. A few minutes during which he'd ended up thinking about the Catie situation instead.

"Here," Eileen said, and put a hard candy in his hand. "Get your blood sugar up. This is a good day, Jake."

"Thank you," he said. He didn't know what else to do but pop the candy in his mouth. Eileen always reminded him of who he had been when he'd first known her—a lonely, emotionally stunted little boy, grasping desperately at the facsimile of a family he found in his father and half-brother, totally ignorant of the fact that he was intruding on Eileen's actual family. Back then she'd openly resented him for the time he'd demanded from her husband and her son. Her familiarity with him now put him on the defensive. After all, all they shared was a history best forgotten and a tragedy neither of them would ever forget. A tragedy that he was partially responsible for. And yet here she was, worrying about his blood sugar and throwing candies at him. It was confusing.

And she'd wanted to see the building that would house the new expansion of Stephan's House. How was he to say no?

"This it?" she asked, looking up at the six-story brownstone. The weather had relented for at least the day, leaving the skies overcast. The clouds looked heavy, and the cold threatened snow.

"Yes," he said. "It's not ready yet, I warned you. Don't judge it too harshly."

"Oh, hush. Go on," she said, gesturing up the stairs.

He led her into the darkened building, flipping on the lights in what was once a sitting room. It would eventually be a reception area, but right now it was just a hollow shell.

"You weren't kidding," she said.

"I tried to tell you there wouldn't be much to see." The candy was a caramel, and it stuck to the roof of his mouth. Now he sounded like a kid, too.

"Some of the girls told me this one would have a fancy photo lab," she said casually.

Jake stiffened. It would. Stephan had been passionate about photography and writing. Jake had done the research: the arts could provide a useful form of occupational therapy. It had seemed like a natural thing to do, but he hadn't envisioned Eileen Corrigan standing in the middle of a construction site, being reminded of her dead son's favorite things.

Not for the first time, he didn't know how to feel.

"I think it can help some people," he finally said.

"Good," she said firmly. "Show me what you're gonna do."

He took her on a brief tour, explaining how many extra beds they'd have, how many staff members, what programs they hoped to offer. The speech had become mechanical by now, and Jake felt his mind begin to wander, as it did, back to Catie. It felt no more odd to think about her in this context than in any other, which in and of itself was odd. She left him completely unsettled. He had come to think that they would move beyond training, into yet some other uncharted territory — a thought which, for him, was nothing short of revolutionary — and then she'd worn the collar he'd given her and promptly disappeared. Not disappeared entirely, but he hadn't seen much of her the past few days. Granted, he was busy — very busy — with Stephan's House, and she seemed to have her own responsibilities. He knew Roman had assigned her something to do with the Valentine's Auction, and he presumed she was very busy with her studies. Her thesis. The thesis for which he would need to do his own homework.

But he couldn't shake the feeling that she was avoiding him. He didn't understand it. Everything about their interactions felt new and incomprehensible to him. He wondered if this was what it was like for normal people, all the time. Is this what it was like to become attached? To feel close? He wasn't sure he could recommend it. And he wasn't sure he could trust it, either.

Just the thought that something might be happening inside him — something he couldn't control — worried him.

And still, his primary responsibility was to Catie. He had promised to complete her training, to help hcr, to discover whatever it was that tormented her, whatever it was she hid, and…well, what she did with it was her own choice. But the process of self-discovery was inseparable from the process of training, and he'd managed to make it, instead, about his own confused feelings.

Feelings. He had them, and he didn't recoil from her. Even when they weren't in a scene, he felt the connection. Unlike anything else he'd ever experienced, it made him feel like he was losing his mind.

"Earth to Jake," Eileen said. She waved a hand in front of his face. "What is up with you?"

"Sorry," he mumbled.

"Girl trouble?" she said. Eileen raised an eyebrow, but she looked pleased.

This was the last thing he needed.

"Of course not," he said, perhaps too quickly.

Yes, too quickly. Eileen gave a cunning smile. "That Catie girl I met, then?"

He didn't know what to say. He just stared at her, stupidly. How did women *do* that?

"You don't bicker like that with people who don't matter," Eileen said confidently, patting his arm as if they were...close. "You just ignore them. Having problems?"

What could he say? Yes, there were problems, problems of the variety he couldn't speak about with his dead father's widow. But it was more than that: there was a problem with this conversation, with the way that Eileen spoke to him in those confidential tones, with the fact that she was attempting to share anything with him beyond what was necessary. Jake felt the old, familiar revulsion start to creep up his spine, and his heart dropped.

He'd had almost a vacation from it, with Catie. It was like they communicated on the same damaged frequency, something that came in under the radar, that fooled his poisoned mind, at least temporarily. When he might have otherwise felt sick at the pretense of affection, there was the D/s dynamic to channel it away. But he wasn't cured.

This was the proof. Eileen Corrigan tried to have a normal conversation with him, something that demonstrated she cared—could she, really? Was anyone that forgiving?—and here was the old reaction.

How long until it manifested around Catie, too?

How long until he hurt her?

"I don't want to talk about it," he said finally.

"It could do you good."

"No."

Eileen nodded. They were standing in the room that would become the photo lab, and Jake felt that the tour had come to an end. Wordlessly, he turned around and started back down the stairs.

He held open the door for Eileen and waited. She stood still in the dark vestibule and peered up at him.

"I want to spend the anniversary with you," she said, her jaw set. "Go out to dinner. Try to remember nice things."

He was flabbergasted. For five years he'd buried himself in what work was available, read Stephan's old letters, avoided Eileen's letter—singular, like the telltale heart that it was—and then drunk himself to sleep watching his movies. This year, the anniversary coincided with the Volare Valentine's Auction, and he'd thought that the festivity of the Auction might perhaps prove enough of a distraction to give him a reprieve. Not that he deserved it. But dinner with Eileen Corrigan on the anniversary of Stephan's suicide?

"I don't understand," he said lamely.

Eileen walked past him into the grey light of early February and looked up at the sky to see if it

174

would rain again.

"I have some things I want to give you," she said. "Some stuff I want you to hear. Try something different, rather than just being miserable. You're screwing up your life with this, you know. It's getting ridiculous."

He felt twelve years old again. "What?"

She rolled her eyes. "So we're on for the fourteenth. We'll go to Angelo's in the old neighborhood. Fantastic, that's settled."

She walked briskly down the steps, looking down the street to see if she could spot a cab. One started to turn the corner, and she walked out into the street with her hand up like the native New Yorker she was.

"Listen," she called back as the cab slowed to a stop. "Will you talk to that girl already? Jesus, Mary, and Joseph, you're gonna screw that up, too. Promise me, all right?"

Without waiting for a response, Eileen ducked into the cab shaking her head, her bright red bob bouncing back and forth. It was just as well. Jake was too stunned and disoriented to be of much use. He stood there, in the middle of the sidewalk, Eileen's final words echoing inside his mind, until he realized she was right: he was going to screw it up. He had made it all about himself, when it was about Catie. And if there was one thing the memory of Stephan made abundantly clear, it was that he couldn't make the mistake of allowing anyone to depend upon him ever again.

He'd have to complete Catie's training, somehow find a way to disentangle the threat of her thesis, and he had to do it quickly, before the stakes grew any larger.

It meant he needed to know more about Catie than she was willing to tell him. It meant he needed to do some investigation. And he knew just who to call.

chapter 18

Catie sat in the Volare lounge and stared morosely at the blue folder in front of her. It was the same blue folder that held all the information on the Volare members and the Valentine's Auction. *Names. Biographical details. Shit they're into.* She took out the New York Lottery scratch ticket she'd bought on the way over and put it on the low table next to the folder, as though it were a viable second option.

Well, you never knew.

She'd gotten another call from Brazzer. Of course she had. She'd been able to delude herself into a fantasy life with Jake at his incredible townhouse for all of one day — one incredible day — before Brazzer had ripped her out of the clouds and pulled her back down to reality. Catie had been disappointed when Jake left her in her own room, with her own bed, but Brazzer's call later that night had reminded her that she needed all the cover—and all the protection—she could get.

Brazzer had wanted to know if she was ever going to have anything for him, or if he should spend the money elsewhere. Catie had tried to get him to give up some info on his alleged second source, but he'd only laughed at her. She'd had to tell him she'd have something for him, but he hadn't believed her. In the end, she'd had to tell him about the auction. Not details, but that it existed. She felt terrible.

And here she was, with the mother lode of gossip information staring her in the face. She'd done what she was supposed to do, she'd written the copy for the Auction catalog. She'd kept a copy of the document for herself, as...she wanted to say as insurance, but it wasn't that. It was so she'd have something to sell Brazzer if she could ever bring herself to pull the trigger. Theoretically, she could do it now. She could call Brazzer up and be out of town tomorrow.

"Shit," she said. There was no one around to hear it. Mid-morning, mid-week—not a busy time at Volare. She was just waiting to meet Lola.

Lola, who made her feel terrible without even meaning to. She couldn't decide if Lola suspected her or worried about her or both.

Catie eyed the lottery ticket again. It was, obviously, stupid. No one wins the lottery. But she couldn't help herself. She'd walk past the bodega and find herself fantasizing about suddenly having the money. She'd be able to call up Ridge Hill and set her grandmother up for the rest of her life, and then she imagined herself tearfully confessing to Jake, and in this fantasy he was angry, but he saw, in the end, how sorry she was, and he understood and he forgave her. And so did everyone else.

It was *beyond* pathetic.

Still, she leapt forward with sudden vehemence and scratched furiously at the silver foil with her nail.

Nope. Loser.

"Did you win?"

She looked up, startled. It was Vincent Duran. Looking at her curiously. Like he was trying to place her.

Catie told herself she was just being paranoid, and forced a smile. "Never do," she said. "What are you doing here?"

They were totally alone.

Vincent unbuttoned his shiny grey suit—this one had a definite sheen to it—and sat down with his arms spread wide on the back of the armchair. He looked at her, smiling, smacking his gum. Like Brazzer had.

"I came to see you," he said.

"I'm here to meet Lola," she said. "I have the catalog stuff. Is she not coming?"

Vincent shook his head, still smiling at her, a puzzled smile.

"I swear to God, I *know* you from somewhere," he said. "It's been driving me crazy. Help a guy out, would ya?"

Catie shrugged helplessly, tried not to overdo it.

"I got nothing," she said.

"Well, *that* ain't true," he said, looking at her

appreciatively.

Catie made a point of fingering the fine leather collar on her neck. She wore it as a choker. Had no idea what it meant, if anything, just that she was training with Jake. That she was his, for the time being. That maybe Vincent better back off.

He seemed to get the message.

"Well, I'll give that stuff to Lola," he said, getting up and rebuttoning his suit jacket. He reached out his hand.

"Are you sure?"

"Yeah, I'm sure. Jesus." He snapped his fingers. Catie had been neutral on him up until that moment. Now Vincent Duran had moved firmly into the "douchebag" category. Reluctantly, she gave him the folder and waited for him to leave.

He didn't. He was still looking at her.

"Is there something else?" This time, she allowed a hint of irritation to seep into her voice. She should just leave. The problem was that she had nowhere to go but Jake's, and she didn't think she would be any better at facing him.

"You remember that trouble I mentioned—the thing with the tabloids?" he said.

"Vaguely," she answered. She felt overheated. Claustrophobic.

"Well, I'm still on it, but I'm not having as much luck as I thought, you know? It's that rag *Sizzle*, so you know what kinda story they're gonna do. I mean, Christ. I know these people from my day job, so I'm working on it. I got a source and I'm gonna nail it, but with the auction coming up, I just wanna tell you to keep an eye out, all right?"

"Will do," she said. She had to get the hell out of

there. She got up, all set to make a beeline for the exit.

"I mean, you'd mention it if anything came up, right?" he said.

Could he tell she was avoiding looking at him?

"Of course I would. Listen, Vincent, I've gotta go. I was just here to meet Lola. Sorry."

Catie smiled and gave him a little wave, and started to walk as fast as possible for the coatroom.

"Yeah, all right, no problem. Hey," he called after her, and it sounded like he was smiling, like he was being friendly, even flirting. "I'm gonna figure out where I know you from, I swear! It's driving me nuts!"

Catie winced.

chapter 19

Catie had no idea what was in store for her back at Jake's townhouse, but she couldn't shake the feeling that she was running out of time.

She spent the rest of the day in the main branch of the New York Public Library, tucked away in the farthest corner of the Rose Room, trying to write out a draft of the story she was supposed to give to Brazzer. She'd always been a good writer, and she'd been confident in her ability to deliver. But she'd only ever fed Brazzer little gossipy tidbits, stuff overheard on bar shifts or on auditions that she could turn into hot little items. Never something like this. Never something she actually cared about, never something that mattered.

It was freaking *hard*. Worse, she felt insanely paranoid after Vincent had put the fear of exposure in her, and so she'd hunch over her notebook any time someone came near her spot, all the way at the end of one of the long tables. It put her on edge as she struggled to try to capture the essence of Volare, what made it special. Every time she felt like she got close, she'd feel guilty all over again. She was a mess.

Eventually, she gave up. She would have to buckle down at some point, but she felt strongly that something was missing, and she preferred to believe it was something she could fix. She'd nearly chewed her way through her pencil when she'd remembered about Jake's once-promising academic career. Professor Jayson. He'd written a book, a well-received, well-reviewed book, right before he'd disappeared completely from the public eye. About five years ago. The sort of thing that might give her the insight she needed to do him justice.

It was easy enough to find. And it made for fascinating reading.

Love and Shakespeare.

She read until closing, and when the lights flickered above her and she finally came up for air, she felt like she'd been right back inside Jake's head. She was nearly out of breath. She was almost relieved to stop, to get a break, until she remembered that she had nowhere to go but back to Jake's.

"I am *such* a crazy person," she muttered.

February had finally settled into its customary bitter chill, and she found herself practically running down the long avenue blocks, her head down against the vicious wind, on the way to Jake's townhouse. She was so caught up in the cold she forgot to be anxious, right up until she was confronted with Jake's insane security system.

He'd given her her own code. He'd programmed her fingerprint into the system. Every time she opened the door, she thought about how much he'd trusted her, how much that meant to her, and how much she didn't deserve it.

The door swung open and Catie hurried inside, stamping her feet on the cold marble floor. She'd meant to hurry up to her room, hide, figure out what to do next. They hadn't even talked about how long she was supposed to stay here, probably because he guessed she didn't have any other options. The whole situation was strange, and felt like it couldn't last. She needed time to think.

But Jake was waiting.

"Oh, come *on*," she whispered. He had just emerged from a room in the back. She hadn't had much chance to explore most of the house. He was dressed in his usual tailored suit, this one a three piece. His dark hair was brushed back, accentuating that early silver streak. He was gorgeous.

"I've been waiting for you," he said.

"I was at the library," she said. That, at least, was true.

He nodded, and she thought she saw a shadow pass across his face at the reminder of her "studies." Her "thesis." She had gotten away with remarkably little questioning on that front; now she wondered if her luck was running out.

"Follow me," he said, and beckoned to her.

Catie glanced down at her bag, which held the notebook full of Volare notes and drafts of her exposé. Just holding it in his presence made her nervous. She desperately wanted to go squirrel it away somewhere where it wouldn't remind her of what she was doing so she could once again lose herself in Jake's presence. She craved that release now more than ever.

"Now," he said, and his tone was one that she recognized. She felt a twinge between her legs and fingered the thin leather collar around her neck, then followed him up the stairs.

He led her to a formal dining room. The south wall was nearly entirely windows, looking out on the snow covered garden, and the long wooden table was lit by a single, large candelabra. It was breathtaking, in a dramatic *Beauty and the Beast* sort of way. She giggled, half expecting the candlestick to start singing at her, and then realized that the strain of leading a double life might be having more of an effect than she'd thought. Giggling probably wasn't the appropriate response.

"Sorry," she said. "I'm just..."

"You seem nervous," he said, taking off his suit jacket. He rolled up the sleeves of his white shirt in his habitual way, and Catie was once again distracted. The man looked amazing in his vest and rolled up cuffs, straight out of a photo shoot or something.

"I am, actually. Nervous." She was getting to tell the truth left and right. It felt good. *Too bad it can't last.* "What is all of this?"

"This," he said, pushing a service tray out from the side of the room, where it had escaped her notice, "is the setting for our next session. And you will address me as 'sir' in session, Catie."

Catie blanched. She had begged him to continue to train her, and at the time she'd meant it. And she *did* need him physically, she did need those moments they shared, whatever they were, even if she preferred not to think about why, or what would happen when it had to end. But in the days since he'd put that collar on her, she'd worried about what he'd told her about training in their very first session: it was about self-discovery. It meant he had to know her better than she knew herself. It meant it was about uncovering secrets.

Which was the last thing she needed. Except, of course, that she did need it. Of course. Nothing about this was simple.

He was looking at her, waiting, his eyes glowing over the candelabra. Just that look was enough to get her blood flowing.

Who was she kidding?

"Yes, sir," she finally said, and as she did, she felt the familiar rush race through her body. His eyes glittered, and she thought she saw him smile. Even though she knew she'd have to fight to keep her secrets, she couldn't wait to see what he was going to do to her.

"Come here," he said.

She put her bag down, nestled against the wall by the door, and hoped it would be forgotten. It took her a moment to take off all her winter stuff and hang it all on the back of one of the antique chairs, but eventually she made it over to his side. He watched her the whole time.

She looked down at the service tray. It was one of two—another was lined up against the wall, waiting. Both had silver service sets.

"So...?"

He grinned. "I want to see how you manage service," he said.

Catie opened her mouth to object—service was about the last thing she imagined herself to be good at—but she was, again, distracted. Jake had started to unbutton her blouse.

"Service?" she said weakly. He whipped her shirt over her shoulders, and the fabric made a sharp snapping sound. He let it fall to the floor, and then removed her collar.

"Service is about mindfulness," he said. "About putting yourself in mind of someone else. Done correctly, it leaves no room for anything else. But given the way your mind works, I've decided to incentivize your performance a bit."

"The way my mind works?" she said, her voice a little arch. He paused, his hands on her bra clasp, and waited. "Sir," she added.

Now he smiled and her bra fell to the floor, joining her shirt in a pile at her feet. He quickly pinched her nipples, and she cried out in surprise. "I think you know what I mean," he said.

She did. In fact, her mind was already going into overdrive. What the hell did he mean by "incentivize?"

Catie didn't have to wait long to find out. Jake lingered over her breasts for a moment, and then looked down at the silver service. He lifted the domed cover to reveal another collar, this one with wires attached. Some of the wires were connected to little metal clamps.

She expected him to explain, but he didn't say anything at all. Instead he picked up a little bottle and squirted something onto his fingers. He rubbed them together as he looked her up and down.

"I think I want you naked," he said, smiling again. "Yes. Take off the rest of your clothes."

She was going to serve him dinner, naked. Catie had never thought of this before, had never had the imagination, apparently, to envision herself in such a servile role. She was surprised to find that it turned her on.

She stripped out of the rest of her clothes, and came up smiling, already wet just from the thrill of being naked with a fully clothed man.

Jake grabbed her nipples, his fingers wet with some kind of cold gel, and rubbed.

She shrieked.

"What the hell is that?" she said. "Sir?"

Jake laughed softly to himself. "This is so the electrodes don't burn you."

"The what now?"

But he was already attaching the new collar to her neck. It was thicker than the previous one, and she felt the weight of heavy grounding cord trailing off behind her. The wires dangled down the front of her chest.

She closed her eyes. "This is…"

"An incentive."

chapter 20

He showed her a little gadget he held in his hand, and she saw that it was a remote control. So that's how he would do it. She licked her lips as he stowed the remote in his pocket.

"An incentive," she repeated. "Positive or negative, sir?"

Jake chuckled. "Well, that remains to be seen. I'd wager both."

"Both?"

He didn't answer. "Two points of contact on each nipple," he explained. "To keep the current local, so it doesn't pass through your ribcage." Catie felt the cold metal clamps on both her nipples, felt them bite into her flesh. She opened her eyes to find him looking at her in open appreciation.

"God, you are beautiful," he said, low enough that she barely heard. He didn't seem to be saying it to her. It meant that much more. Now she felt truly naked.

"I'll want you to serve me dinner," he said, barely able to tear his eyes away from her body. "But as you can probably deduce, that will only be your nominal activity."

"Whatever you say, sir."

She felt overheated, already. She kept thinking about the electrodes on her nipples. What on earth would that feel like? When would he do it? How? That he was drawing it all out was killing her.

He suddenly turned, pulled out the chair at the head of the impressive table, and sat down languidly.

"I'm hungry," he said, motioning toward the other service cart with a knowing smile. "And thirsty."

Catie felt the beginnings of a tremor deep inside. This was a new level of submission, for her, and it...

She shivered.

"Yes, sir."

What did he mean about mindfulness? It was difficult to think about anything else but him, reclining as he was in those fitted trousers, looking at her. And she was *naked*, with freaking electrodes attached to her nipples. How was she supposed to think about anything else but when he would activate them? When he would touch her? When would he finally —

"Wine first, I think," he called out.

She snapped to attention and saw that there was

a bottle of Chianti on the lower shelf of the second service cart, already opened, presumably breathing for the requisite half hour. Next to it was a set of fine crystal wine glasses. Hesitantly, she walked towards it.

"You can do better than that," he said.

Her spine straightened. She was, at first, more offended than anything. Catie thought she might be a lot of things — spoiled, entitled, naïve, apparently capable of the worst betrayal — but she had, at the very least, always strived to be the best at whatever she did. Mindfulness. She hadn't been mindful. She hadn't been conscious of the act of walking, she hadn't thought about what it looked like to him.

Well, he wanted mindful? She would knock his socks off.

She bent over, arching her back slightly, just to give him something to think about, and retrieved the bottle of wine and one glass. This she walked over to the table, her carriage erect, her breasts thrust forward. The posture alone made her more aroused.

The bastard knew what he was doing.

He watched her pour the wine with a satisfied smile.

"Very nice," he said as she held the bottle correctly, turning it as she finished the pour.

"I've been to nice restaurants, sir."

"But not everybody notices their servers."

That was true. She was quite accustomed to being treated like a piece of meat at most of the bars where she'd worked.

"I have a feeling you do, sir."

He took the wine without another word, and swirled a sip in his mouth. It looked good. *He* looked good. His mouth looked good.

She was getting distracted again.

"Who is your thesis advisor?" he said suddenly.

She stopped short, the bottle poised in the air. She was completely unprepared for that. Which was ridiculous—she should have been prepared for exactly that. That he hadn't asked before was a small miracle. She blinked, licked her lips, put the bottle down.

She was just about to say something—anything—when she felt the first shock.

It started as just a low tingle on her nipples, starting there and shooting straight to her spine, and grew to a cacophonous buzzing, nearly painful, just before it stopped. It did stop, but it left a powerful echo. Her body roared, the sensation centered now on her clit, her nipples slightly burning. She gripped the edge of the table.

"Sir," she managed.

"Incentive," Jake said, raising one hand to reveal the tiny remote.

"I'm not comfortable answering that," she said, improvising. Her nipples still tingled, and she was wet, slick between the thighs. It was hard to think straight.

"Why not?" he said.

"You having a chat with my thesis advisor? It could compromise me."

Now Jake smiled broadly, showing off that million-dollar smile. It was a crime that he could be so gorgeous right now. She had enough working against her.

"So you're drawing a boundary?" he asked. "What you might call a 'hard line?'"

She smiled too, but she could feel that hers was weak.

"Yes," she said. "Sir. I did ask you to help me find them."

"That you did." He took another drink of his wine, his eyes once again trailing down the length of her body, and up again, to meet her gaze. "Incredible. You have no idea, do you? And yet, there's something you're not telling me."

She laughed in spite of herself. "Everyone has something they don't tell people," she said. She looked him dead in the eye, and she'd never know why she did what she did next. "Even you, Mr. Know Yourself. Sir."

He met her gaze, evenly. Didn't move a muscle, not even the hand that held the remote.

"But this isn't about me," he said.

She laughed again. Catie didn't know why, but with the presence of the electrodes, or maybe just the situation she was in — whatever it was — she felt let loose. Not drunk, but not sober. Dangerous.

She was still laughing softly. She could tell by his expression that he couldn't quite figure out what was going on.

"Oh my God, with this again?" she said finally, and poured him some more wine. He was probably going to need it. "How can it not be about you, too? You're here, right? You're participating."

He seemed sort of stunned.

"If you say it's not personal again I'm going to scream, I swear," she said, plunking the bottle on the table. She had no idea what had gotten into her.

She was going way off script; she was messing with the scene. She was demanding honesty, of a sort, from someone she was determined to lie to. It was like the world's greatest bluff.

Holy crap, had she rendered Jacob Jayson actually speechless? He laughed. He stared. She had no idea what impelled her to keep going.

"I read your book," she said. She was just desperate now, casting about for things that weren't about her. This one appeared to work.

"What?" he said, suddenly serious. He leaned forward, his little remote control apparently forgotten.

"Yeah, *Love and Shakespeare*," she said, filling his glass to the glistening brim just to give her hands something to do, her voice shaking the entire time. "Kind of weird for a guy who says he can't become attached. Like, interesting area of study. I liked the sonnets you quoted," she added at the end, stupidly. The damage was already done, even if it was true.

He said nothing. Just stared at her. She felt the urge to go further on the offensive, in a last, desperate surge. Maybe it would even work.

"And you know what else I've been thinking about?" she said, putting the bottle down, aware, again, of her nakedness, yet unable to keep herself from talking. "What is up with the bartending? I mean, everyone at Volare probably knows who you are, except, obviously, dumb people like me. It's not like you're incognito. But you make such a point of it," she rattled on, wishing she could stop. What the hell was wrong with her? "It's not like you need the money."

Now she just stood in front of him, naked, with those electrodes on her. She felt like she'd gone too far. She felt it was obvious, what she was doing: deflecting. Making it about him.

She felt this was how she'd be caught.

But he answered. He studied her, he calculated, he toyed with the remote in his hand. But he answered.

"My father was a bartender," he said. Not ashamed, not angry. Just...evenly. Watching her. "That's how my parents met. He was tending bar on a chartered yacht, and my mother was...my mother. He tracked her down when he saw in the papers that she was pregnant."

She didn't know what to say, exactly, except to press her point. Be investigative. God, what was she thinking?

"So, like, in memoriam?"

"Not exactly. But I try to be more like him than like her. I remember him most taking care of people in his bar."

Jake paused, turning to his glass of wine. He took a long, slow, memorial sort of drink.

"I'm sorry," she said. "I know I'm prying but...your life is so weird. And you keep asking me questions, and it's just weird not to know about you."

Oh, Christ, what was she doing? He pushed his chair away from the table and turned it to face her. Then he took her hand and pulled her close, between his legs. Her skin felt hot, and she could feel the focus shifting back to her, back to his questions. His calm stare did nothing to help her feel more in control.

"So what about that book?" she asked. It sounded forced, even to her.

"This was about you," he said. He still held the remote in one hand. With the other, he began to trace designs on her stomach. She couldn't hide how she quivered every time he touched her there.

She couldn't believe she'd pressed the point. Not because she was supposed to be serving him, though that struck her as incongruous. Not because they had this strangely regimented relationship. But because as she looked at him, it became clear that no one, ever, had forced him to answer this particular question.

It suddenly struck her: it was possible he'd never been forced to answer any question, ever. Certainly not by a naked girl with electrodes attached to her nipples.

"It won't work, Catie," he said. "What you're doing right now. There's something you're hiding. Something you're afraid of."

"And if there was?"

"There is. And I'm going to find out what."

Jake held up the remote and pressed the button.

chapter 21

Jake watched Catie writhe between his legs and felt himself harden even more, if that were possible. She made it so difficult to maintain focus, to pursue a goal with any kind of consistency. It was all he could do to keep from throwing her on that table. And that was what he was supposed to do to her: distract to her the point where she didn't have the wherewithal to lie, to hide, to avoid.

He pressed the button again, and she twisted her hands into the fabric of his trousers and moaned.

Jake knew what she was doing it. It confirmed what he'd thought about the way she reacted to vulnerability. Every time he got close, she'd push him away by testing some boundary, and pull him in by provoking him. That dance was intoxicating.

Maybe it was what drew him to her. Maybe it was what let him feel.

"Oh God, Jake!"

He took his thumb off the button and she leaned over him, arms on his shoulders. His buried his face between her breasts and inhaled. He was starting to lose it.

He held her as she shook, waiting for her to regain just enough strength to answer his questions, just not enough to avoid them. But he misjudged her. Again.

"So about that book," she said into his ear, laughing weakly.

How could he not admire a woman like that?

Jake ran his free hand down the side of her body, let himself cup her wonderful ass. He sighed.

"I told you I cannot become attached or emotionally involved," he said, moving his hand around to the front of her thigh. "But I didn't always accept that. I…studied it, with an aim towards acquiring the ability. Like you would a technical skill."

"And how'd that work out for you?" she breathed.

He pushed his hand between her legs, burying it in the warm wetness between her thighs. She was unbelievably wet. He decided to tease her some more, and flicked twice at her swollen outer lips. She jumped.

He said, "It didn't."

She remained silent. Her breath was quick and shallow, and hot on his ear. He pulled her off his shoulders and moved his legs between hers, opening her so that she straddled him. Her eyes were half-closed and her skin was flushed, her collarbone glinting with a thin sheen of sweat, but she still had that spark.

"Catie," he said. "No matter what you do, you won't evade me. I'll find out. I'll get you to *tell* me. I'll get you to beg to tell me."

He balanced her on his legs, her own legs spread wide for him, and pushed the button.

Catie arched her back and screamed. He watched the muscles in her abdomen flex and strain, and when he could see she was on the verge of an orgasm, he stopped.

She whipped her head back to look at him, blinking, confused. She was shaking.

"Please…" she said. "Let me come."

"No."

"Please!"

He shoved his free hand back between her legs, and thrust two fingers inside of her, saying, "Don't come, Catie." Her muscles squeezed him tight, and she moaned, leaning into him again.

"Please, Jake," she whispered. "I can't…"

"What are you afraid will happen if I know you too well, Catie?" he asked.

Her hips had started to rock on his hand, almost unconsciously, and she leaned back again so he could see her face. She looked tortured, tired, torn, and yet balanced on the precipice of something amazing, something big. He felt guilty, felt terrible, felt actual pain—he didn't want to make her feel anything bad, ever. But then he watched her face. He watched her turn her fear around, as he'd seen her do before, watched her confront whatever it was. Watched her be brave.

She looked him in the eye, her face soft, her hips rocking gently. "I'm afraid if you know me too well, then you won't want to know me at all," she said.

Jake didn't understand what was happening to him. He looked at her, looked at the jumbled swirl of emotions, plain as day on her face, and he felt them inside. It was like a storm had broken in his chest, and it was frightening. He was feeling what he saw in her, he was *feeling*, period, with another person, in the moment, like the live line that connected them had given him a sense of empathy, a way to feel, vicariously. Years of being unable to do exactly this had left him wholly unprepared.

"Oh Jesus," he said.

A beat.

He removed his hand and tore at his belt buckle at the same moment she went for his zipper, the two of them fumbling like idiots, finally managing to free his aching cock. She didn't wait for him, just wrapped her arms around his neck to pull herself forward and then lowered herself onto him, groaning as she slid down the full length of his cock.

Jake wrapped his hands around her hips and pushed up into her, loving the expression on her face, loving that he put it there. She picked up the rhythm, grinding into him, and when she opened her eyes to look down at him, he decided to see how high he could push her.

"Come for me," he said.

And he pressed the button.

Catie screamed, coming violently around his dick, bucking and thrashing in his lap. Jake dug his fingers into the flesh of her hips in the effort to hold back, to keep himself going. He didn't want it to end. Sweat dripped down his forehead into his eyes, and his shirt stuck to his chest as Catie writhed in his lap, shivering, shaking, her hot, wet flesh quivering around his. She collapsed with her arms around him, twitching once, twice. He couldn't wait for her aftershocks to pass. He dug his hands under her thighs and rose, lifting her up, and placed her on the table. He was still hard; he still wanted her more than anything. He climbed on top of her, and brushed her hair away from her face.

He had pulled out of her, and now he positioned himself right above her, poised to enter her again. He was determined to go slow, determined to show her how grateful he was for whatever it was that had just happened to him, for whatever it was she had made possible in him, since he didn't think he'd ever figure out how to tell her.

"Keep coming," he whispered. "You let me know when you've had enough."

He slid into her slowly and deeply, and when he was fully in, he bent down to remove the clamps with his teeth. He wanted her nipples for himself. She moaned again, a sound he loved, as he took one and then the other into his mouth, nibbling softly while she arched her back.

When he started to move again, she moaned with him, and he couldn't stop himself from looking at her face. He lost count of how many times she came, of what were full-blown orgasms and what were just the shuddering gasps of her worn out body, but finally he felt he couldn't hold out any longer. With one last, hard thrust, he let himself go.

He didn't know how long they lay atop his ruined table. Didn't care, really. He'd fallen on his back, spent, and Catie had rolled over to lie on his chest, as though they did this all the time. In the back of his mind, he knew this was significant, too, but it wasn't until Catie propped herself up on his chest, her eyes clear now, steady, though it looked like she might have cried, and leaned forward to kiss him that he knew something had changed — changed utterly.

"I think I know you too well," she said softly, and leaned her head back into his neck.

The thing was, Jake wasn't repulsed at this intimate affection. He didn't recoil. Instead, he felt a sweetness blossoming in him, a desire to bring Catie more moments just like this. He had crossed the rubicon, in a way, and wouldn't be the same. And he'd done it for it a woman who was hiding something from him.

chapter 22

"I was afraid you would still be angry with me," Roman said, deftly picking up a piece of uni with his chopsticks. Roman had invited Jake to dinner...in his Volare office. Roman valued privacy, and had a good relationship with a sushi restaurant that delivered without asking too many questions.

"I am," Jake said.

"And yet?"

"Even when wrong, you may occasionally be right," Jake said, sipping at his whiskey. He did enjoy Roman's taste in whiskey. "So here I am."

Roman grinned wolfishly. "So something has happened, then?"

Jake laughed without any real mirth. "Yes. I have crossed every line of impropriety with respect to Catie. Every single one. Without even...That is to say, I am not accustomed..."

Jake shook his head, unable to find the words. Roman was smiling now, broadly.

"Don't look so happy," Jake snapped. "I've done her a real disservice. I have no idea what the consequences might be. I—"

"Relax, Jacob," Roman said. "It is natural for human beings to have defenses. But then how do people ever grow close unless they cross these lines?"

Jake didn't have an answer to that. He didn't have much experience with the normal progression of intimacy. He had no frame of reference.

"It is a conundrum," Roman allowed. Jake remembered that Lola had gotten him a Word of the Day calendar, and chuckled. Roman had scoffed at it, said his English vocabulary was fine. Apparently Jake wasn't the only man susceptible to the subtle influence of a woman.

"Are you going to tell me about it?" Roman said.

"You can tell that something has happened?" Jake asked. The idea made him uncomfortable.

"Something, yes. Something good?"

Jake sat silently. He wasn't hungry. He'd been...perturbed, since his last "session" with Catie. He couldn't even properly call it a session. It had turned completely on its head—*she* had turned it completely on its head. Jake couldn't identify exactly what had happened to him, what had changed, but he had noticed it had begun to bleed into other areas of his life. Perhaps without realizing it, he had slowly grown accustomed to the idea that things were simply different with Catie, that he was somehow more open with her. He had not grown accustomed to the idea of opening himself up to the world at large.

He hadn't even been properly aware of how guarded he was, of what defenses he had around him, until they'd started to fade. But then there had been a visit from Eileen to confirm their dinner date, and his skin did not crawl. Whether it was simply the residual glow from Catie — God, Catie — or something more profound, he had no way of knowing. And it was driving his analytical mind mad.

But there was nothing analytical about whatever was going on inside him, nothing at all. Jake remembered what he had arrogantly told Catie during their first session: some things just *are*.

Indeed. Just his luck that he would experience something like that with a woman who was hiding something from him.

"Jake?"

Jake looked up. "I apologize, Roman. I am…preoccupied."

"I can see that, my friend. You look worried. Is that correct? Anxious."

Jake scowled. He had been thinking about whether it had been wise to leave Catie the particular present he'd found for her. At the time it had seemed perfect, meaningful, the sort of thing only she would understand. Since then — since only that morning — it had begun to gnaw at him in a most unfamiliar way. He kept thinking back to what Catie had said the first day she'd come to stay with him, when she'd begged him to continue to train her: that she needed it, the same way he did. Unspoken: she, too, was saddled with some heretofore crippling emotional wound, something she hid, something that had scarred over, forming a barrier between her and the world. Perhaps the same thing she hid from him, perhaps not.

Perhaps something that meant his little gesture with the book was too much, too fast. Or perhaps not. And round and round his mind went. It was *maddening*. How did normal people stand this?

Irritated, Jake said, "Roman, this is not a productive area of conversation. If this is why you wanted to have dinner —"

Roman shook his head, spreading his arms. "No, no. Forget it. I do have something to ask of you. The Valentine's Auction."

"What about it?"

"Lola tells me that Lindsey Grunwald has broken her leg skiing, and that this leaves a vacancy in the catalog."

"So?"

"Perhaps Catie could fill the vacancy."

Jake put his drink down. "You want Catie to offer herself up for auction at the Valentine's benefit? To the highest bidder?" He flushed with anger as he thought about what that meant. "No, absolutely not. Out of the question. No. I won't allow it."

Roman laughed, delighted. "But that is not for you to decide, my friend."

"We're not asking you if you'll *sell* her, Jake," Lola's voice came from behind him. "We're asking you if you'll *buy* her. You know, within the limits of the event. And it's not my idea, I might add."

Jake turned to find Lola closing the door behind her. Her usually beatific face was clouded with uncertainty. These two had been up to something, something to which he was not privy.

"Is one of you going to explain this?" he said.

"Roman thinks this is a fantastic opportunity to get Catie more involved," Lola said, perching on the edge of Roman's desk. Roman watched her silently. "He insists, rather."

"I do. I have already asked Catie."

Jake tensed. "You asked her if she'd participate in an auction to the highest bidder?"

"Yes, with certain conditions."

Jake's entire body went cold. As calmly as he could, he said, "And what did she say?"

"The conditions are that you would be the one to buy her, Jake."

He wasn't even embarrassed to be so visibly relieved, not even when he realized this might be a patented Roman move: to show him he cared. He already knew he cared. The idea of Catie going to any other man shut down the logical part of his brain and awakened some frightening, primeval part of him. Not for the first time, he wondered if normal people had to deal with this sort of thing on a regular basis. The way people talked about love, you'd think it was a lot more pleasant than this.

Love.

"Jake, are you all right?"

"I'm fine." He got up, possessed of a desire to be elsewhere. To find a way that everything made sense.

To see Catie.

"So you'll do it?"

"Of course," he said. "Roman, enough of this. It's obvious you have some sort of plan, or ulterior—"

Jake was interrupted by his phone, a specific ringtone that he had assigned to exactly one person, for one purpose.

Captain Seenan.

"Excuse me," Jake said. Normally he would not do this, but this call… Roman raised an eyebrow, but said nothing. Lola looked between the two and sighed.

"Captain."

Captain Seenan's voice was hesitant. Uncomfortable. "Mr. Jayson, I have some preliminary results for that inquiry you asked for. About Catie…Roberts."

"Yes?"

"Well, Roberts isn't her last name."

"What do you mean it's not her last name?" Jake said. He had both Roman and Lola's attention. It was his fault for being rude enough not to leave the room, and from the raised eyebrows, it was clear they knew who he was talking about. "Please explain."

"Well, from what I can piece together," Captain Seenan said, "it has something to do with embezzlement."

Wordlessly, Jake let himself out of Roman's office. He was already walking toward the elevators, already on his way to Catie.

"Tell me everything you've found so far," he said.

chapter 23

Catie hugged her knees, folded herself up on the red leather couch in Jake's library, and stared at that stupid book. She'd read it already, of course, as a kid. It had been one of her father's prop books that he kept around just for appearances: *Crossing the Rubicon*. An historical narrative of Caesar's defining moment, when he led his army across the border, the river Rubicon, from the provinces and into Rome's territory, making his insurrection official and marking the beginning of his coup. He'd famously said, "*alea iacta est*": the die is cast. It had been the point of no return.

And Jake left her a book all about it. A first edition, no less.

Catie had been making herself nuts trying to figure out what he meant by it. What die had been cast? What was the point of no return? No return from *what*?

Did he know?

The idea that he might find out, that she wouldn't be able to explain first, and that he'd think the very worst, made her feel absolutely sick.

Catie had been on edge ever since the last time they'd made love. That's what it had been, even if it had been…unconventional. There was no mistaking it. It was the one honest thing she'd done in recent memory, the only time she was truly herself: when she was naked with Jake.

Pathetic.

And then Roman had called. She was to fill in at the auction, with Jake buying. She didn't fully understand why it was necessary, but she knew how she felt. The idea of Jake standing up and claiming her was…

It was trouble, was what it was. She wanted it too badly. And there was no one who deserved it less than her.

She kept going back to that moment, when she'd told the truth, for once, and he'd looked at her like he loved her. Like he loved her in spite of himself. And she had wanted to believe it, more than anything. She'd wanted to believe she could tell him everything, that she could confess it all, that she could cry her apology to him, tell him how truly, truly sorry she was, and he'd miraculously forgive her. He'd take her in his arms, and together they'd find a way to save Volare from Brazzer's other source. That moment contained every comforting fantasy she'd ever had. She'd wanted to believe she could rely on him to be there, to love her regardless of her mistakes, in spite of everything. It had been the best feeling.

But that's how it always felt before everything went bad. This, Catie supposed, was the hangover. Now she was just scared. Scared, and alone, and in over her head.

And Brazzer kept calling.

While Catie had been sitting in the library, staring at that book that meant who knew what, her phone had begun to vibrate at regular intervals. If there was a better way to lose your mind, Catie didn't want to know about it. She was afraid to move. A decision either way, any positive action on her part, would involve crossing some Rubicon or the other—either she got off her ass and truly committed to trying to save her grandmother by betraying Jake, or she left her Nana out in the cold and tried to do the right thing by Jake and Volare.

The phone started to vibrate again, skidding across the antique end table. She just couldn't bear it anymore.

"Fine! What? What do you want?"

Brazzer sounded lewdly amused. "Am I interrupting anything? Anything I should know about?"

"Just tell me what you want." All of Catie's frustration and fear was coalescing into one big giant ball of anger, and it was aimed at Brazzer. The rational part of her brain knew that this was not smart. She tried to reel it in. "I'm working on it," she said through gritted teeth. "But this is not ideal."

"Yeah, well, you'd better work faster. I gotta go with this story sooner rather than later, and I like what I've got, but I'd like what you've got even more, you understand?"

A chill went through her. She hadn't actually given him anything yet, besides some general background on the Valentine's Auction. She'd been as careful as she could be about that.

"No, I'm afraid I don't," she said. "What is it you think I've got?"

"You got Jacob Jayson, sweetheart," Brazzer crowed. "How come I gotta hear about that from someone else—that Jacob Jayson has been seen with someone matching your lovely description? You got the society playboy who left his brother to die in the gutter and then disappeared to do some charity bullshit, and now he resurfaces in a secret pervert society? You gotta be kidding me. That is newsworthy, believe me. Plenty of dollar signs on that one."

Catie's throat ran dry. She opened her mouth to speak, but thought better of it. The silence seemed to stretch out, time dilating long enough to accommodate every horrible thought that wanted to march through her head.

Left his brother to die? And then disappeared to do charity? What brother?

Stephan's House.

Eileen Corrigan. Jake said her son died.

Catie swallowed. "What do you know about Jacob Jayson?"

"Just what I said. Big scandal, about five years ago, hushed up because his family knows people. Left the kid to die like a dog, his half-brother by his nobody father. Kid was some kind of addict or whatever. But you know these money people, connected up the wazoo, so the New York papers wouldn't touch it. Me, I don't give a shit who he knows, that society crap pulls no weight with me. I want this dirt."

Secrets. Everybody had secrets. Even Jake.

Catie's eyes were drawn to the shelf with Jake's old movies, the movies he'd shown her that first day, the ones he would watch when his mother locked him away like some unwanted mutt. There'd been a leather case back there. Green leather. Something he hadn't wanted her to touch, something he hadn't even wanted her to see. She'd been too distracted by how much she wanted him at the time to think much about it—that was the first time he'd had her in this house, when she'd begged him to train her, when she'd told him she'd needed it just like he did, and the memory made her feel both warm and achingly vulnerable—but now, now that she knew he had a secret, a secret that was possibly even worse than hers, now it was all she could think about. Her head throbbed, and the shelf seemed to pulsate in her vision. She closed her eyes.

"I don't know anything about that," she said mechanically.

"Well, what the fuck do you know?"

Good question. She blanked.

Panicked, Catie dropped her voice to a rushed whisper. "Brazzer, I gotta go. I'll call you when I have something, don't call me."

And she hung up. She was breathing fast, in a room that suddenly seemed very still. Those stupid movies, and the shelf beyond it, had a certain glow. It was difficult to look at anything else.

Catie couldn't even identify all the emotions that churned within her, all the various fears and anxieties and desires that pitched about like so much wreckage of a shattered heart. Jake had kept beating that drum, kept insisting he knew that *she* was the one hiding something. The fact that he'd been right had kept her from wondering how he might know what that looked like. Jake had been hiding, too, all along. The man she'd come to count on without realizing it, just to be himself, just for this one interlude in Catie's otherwise wasted life, had his own secret. Catie really did feel sick now.

Is this what a broken heart felt like?

No. That wasn't fair at all. Wasn't this exactly what she'd just feared would happen to her, with Jake, that he'd find out and she wouldn't have a chance to explain? She wouldn't take *Brazzer's* word for it, that was for damn sure.

But Brazzer seemed to know. And what Brazzer knew…

Catie hesitated for just a moment, and then propelled herself at that shelf like she was afraid she'd never bring herself to do it if she lost the momentum. Maybe this was just a rationalization, but it was another good one: she had to know the truth if she could hope to protect him from Brazzer's exposé. From the exposé she would theoretically help write.

And she just wanted to know. She wanted to know what Jake hid from the world. She wanted to know because she suspected that she would love him no matter what, but there was only one way to be sure.

Love.

Catie stopped just short of that shelf, her fingers balanced on the edge. *Love.* She had managed to tell the truth this time, even if she'd done it by accident, even if she'd only said it to herself.

She was screwed.

Feverishly, Catie ripped out the film canisters, piling them one on top of the other on an antique desk. There was the little green leather case. It didn't even have a lock, just latches. Well, why would he need to lock it? He kept himself alone. All these years, he'd kept himself alone. It was hard not to think he'd been punishing himself. Catie had to wonder if he deserved it.

"All right," she said to herself. "One last fucked up thing. I'll do one last fucked up thing."

Carefully, almost reverently, she took the case and set it on the desk. She worked the latches — they were worn; whatever was in here, he did look at it occasionally — and lifted the lid.

Papers. Lots and lots of papers. No — letters. Almost retro, actual written letters, written with the uneven strokes of a fountain pen on heavy stationary, the kind a big fan of letters would use. All in the same handwriting.

Heart pattering, Catie looked. All of them were signed, "S."

She groaned. Part of her really didn't want to read them. Of all the shady things she'd done over the past few months, this felt by far the most…the most violating. She started almost by accident, catching a stray line, naturally following to see where it led, then another, then another. Obviously, she had meant to do this; obviously, she was choosing to do it, but still, she slipped into it almost unaware.

They were unaccountably sad. Not because they described some great tragedy, but because they were obviously the product of someone who was mentally ill. Or strung out, or both. Variously begging, accusing, laudatory, and insulting, they went on and on and on. Sometimes the writer would ask for money, other times there'd be long, rambling explanations about why he'd quit another program. Some of them were snippets of diary entries—the kinds of thing people do during therapy. Some of them were short stories. All had beautiful, demented turns of phrase.

Catie sat on the floor, and the letters began to fan out around her like petals. The record of a descending life. They were excruciatingly painful to read, taken for what they were, and instead, Catie turned a critical eye to the sorts of references that would tell her what she wanted to know about Jake. From what she could tell, Jake sent this "S"— Stephan, she supposed—to private program after private program, to hospital after hospital. He'd sent money, too, but apparently that had stopped, as the letters bitterly referenced. Catie recognized some of these patterns. She'd dated a cokehead once for about five minutes; she couldn't imagine being related to an addict, with all the manipulative stuff they pulled. Couldn't imagine the heartbreak.

"S" accused Jake of all sorts of things, but what stuck out the most was the accusation that Jake had no compassion. No feeling. No warmth. Catie felt herself getting angry at a dead man—this was where the poisonous lie that Jake had no heart had gained strength. Jake's narcissistic mother had started it, she guessed, and Stephan—or the deranged addict that Stephan had become—knew just how to take advantage of it.

Eventually, the letters stopped.

But there was one more. From a different hand, an older, old-fashioned hand, on ordinary lined paper, ripped out of an ordinary spiral notebook, not the sort of thing someone who revered the written word to the point of fetishization would use. It came with a clipping—a gossip column, a picture of Jake looking blitzed out of his mind, some blonde model on his arm. Catie recognized it as the last public press mention of Jake that she herself had been able to find when she'd gone looking.

Dated about five years ago.

Again, Catie groaned. She almost didn't want to read it, almost didn't want to know, but she plodded on. She looked at the end first. It was signed, "Eileen Corrigan."

And once Catie read it, she couldn't stop. There was one passage she kept returning to, over and over again, like a sore tooth she couldn't stop worrying with her tongue, like something that was so horrible she needed to feel the prick of it, over and over again, just to be sure it was real:

"My boy's suicide note talked about you, Jake. He said if his own brother couldn't stand him, maybe there was something to that. I want you to know that, Jake. He cut me out years ago, but you still had a chance. I want you to know that he killed himself when you gave up on him. I want you to know that this is what you were

doing when he did it. You killed him. Your heartlessness killed him."

Catie's heart seized, and became a painful, twisting knot in her chest, twisting a little further every time she thought about Jake reading those words. They were so unfair, so patently, obviously unfair, and worse still was to think about the mad grief that had driven poor Eileen Corrigan to write them.

Catie couldn't match up the Eileen Corrigan she'd met—the Eileen Corrigan who worked at Jake's charity, the Eileen Corrigan who affectionately bullied him like a nosy aunt—with that damning letter. There was no address, no postmark; it had been hand delivered. At the funeral? Catie shuddered. There was so much pain wrapped up in these letters, so much festering in the deep wound that they represented. One word swam out from amidst all the others, made itself known as Catie sat in the paper ruins of Stephan's short life: *heartless*. It was how Jake had described himself, in so many words. Like he was the tin man, a broken boy, a hollow robot without the ability to grow a human heart. It was total, *total* bullshit, and yet he believed it about himself, and those letters were part of the reason why.

I can't be a part of this. I can't be a part of the world that turns on him, too.

She would tell Brazzer to go fuck himself. She would go to Roman; she would do whatever she could to find out the other source. She would beg Roman to be forgiven, beg that no one else would ever have to know what she'd almost done, least of all Jake. She would do whatever she could to try to show him how wrong that letter was.

Catie was crying for him, crying for Jake in a way that she'd never even really cried for herself, when Jake himself walked in and found her sitting in a pile of his most private papers.

chapter 24

They looked at each other. There was a long silence.

He was wearing his usual black tailored suit, and he had come into the room gently. Perhaps he'd heard her, and what she was doing had dawned on him slowly as he'd approached the room. Perhaps it had slowed him.

He stood there, shocked, possibly, his face curiously expressionless, and took in the scene. Catie didn't try to hide anything, not even her tears. For the first time, she didn't have anything to say.

But Jake did.

"Tell me, Catie," he said, his eyes locked on the letters. "Is what you've read better or worse than what you've been hiding from me?" His voice shook, rumbling on a low register, deep in his chest. She watched him screw up his face, trying to find an expression that fit.

What she'd done—what she'd been caught doing—was just beginning to dawn on her.

"Answer the question," he said, closing the door behind him. "Is what you've read there, in Stephan's letters—" He paused, bringing a hand to his mouth, but managed to keep going. "Is what you've read about me worse than what you've been hiding from me?"

Catie shook her head.

"Answer me!" he yelled. He made a fist, punched the back of the couch, then took a step back, his hand covering his mouth. "I'm sorry. I won't…"

"Don't apologize." Catie said, very quickly. To hear him apologize filled her with self-loathing. She deserved his rage—why wouldn't he be angry?

"You don't have to be afraid of me," Jake choked on the words. "I don't want you to be afraid of me. Even if…" He gestured at the piles of letters, shaking his head. "Catie."

"No," she said, gathering the letters carefully, as though they were precious, treasured things, and not poison. She put them back in the case, and put the case back on the shelf, pointlessly trying to hide them away. "This is not worse. This isn't even bad. You—"

"Don't tell me it isn't bad. It damn well is."

"You should be *angry*," she said. She almost wanted him to do something terrible; maybe she'd feel less guilty if he did something terrible. And yet again, she was thinking about herself. Bitterly, she said, "You should be furious. You should… I *deserve* for you to hate me."

Jake shook his head mutely, eyes wide, staring at her. The distance between them was enormous. She walked toward him, and he backed away. Her heart sank.

"I deserve for you to hate me," she said again. "Why aren't you angry? Why haven't you…"

She didn't want to say it. She knew it wasn't in him, somehow, he wouldn't ever be violent in anger. But that wasn't the worst thing she could imagine. The worst thing she could imagine was that he'd never look at her again.

"Jake, please," she said. "Just say something, anything—"

"I don't hate you," he said slowly. "Because I know why you did this."

Jake's eyes came alight and focused on her, clear as day. His face darkened, and he stopped his retreat. Jaw squared, he walked toward her.

"I know why you did this," he said. "Catie Rose."

Catie found herself unable to move, a gross parody of a paralytic, like it would all become real the moment she broke the stillness.

Jake did it for her.

"Did you hear me?" he said, bending down to get a good look at her face. He wasn't far now, just a few steps. "I said I *know*, Miss Rose."

It broke in on her mind like a giant, crashing wave. He knew? And he didn't hate her? Was that possible? She hadn't really allowed herself to believe that that was a possibility, and now she knew why: she hated herself so thoroughly for what she'd planned to do that she assumed anyone else would, too. Catie looked at Jake for the first time without the effort of a concealment, without worrying about what he might find out, what he would think. For just a second, she smiled at him, completely bare.

But then she studied his face. He was angry, yes, but not nearly angry enough. For the most part he looked…well, grimly triumphant was the only way she could think to put it. He didn't seem wounded, or at least not wounded enough. He was upset, but not with *her*. No man was that understanding. None.

He couldn't know. He couldn't. If he knew, he wouldn't be speaking to her. He wouldn't…would he?

Catie's brain kicked back into gear, and she thought quickly.

"How did you find out my last name?" she said.

"I asked Captain Seenan to look into it."

"You asked Captain Seenan to find out my real name?" she asked, carefully. "What I mean is, how did you know it was…"

"How did I know it was fake in the first place? Because I couldn't find your graduate program."

Catie stiffened. It was ridiculous that she should be offended that he'd try to find out about her completely fake graduate program, but it was the one limit she'd set. "I told you I wasn't comfortable with that."

Jake laughed in disbelief, and spread his arm in a wide arc. "Did you think I would be comfortable with you going through my ancient history? That that's why I had it all hidden away, because I was so comfortable with it?"

"I'm sorry," she said. "I had to."

It was the only thing she could think to say.

"I know you had to, Catie," Jake said softly. He took another step toward her, and an arc of sodium-tinted light from the quiet street fell across his face and chest, making him very hard to read. Her heart beat out a staccato rhythm, and she almost didn't dare to breathe.

"Why did I have to?" she asked. It was barely a whisper.

He was close enough to touch her now. She felt his fingertips on her bare forearm, and she jumped.

"I've watched you," he said. "I've watched you in our sessions. Whenever I get close to you, whenever I learn something, you push me back like this. You rifle through my wallet, you go through my personal correspondence. You violate some boundary. You provoke me and you push me away. I didn't know why until I found out about your father."

Catie cleared her throat and kept her voice very even. This was important. "What did you find out?"

"He stole from you. Abandoned you. What I know is probably only the most visible manifestation of his failure. I imagine it did not start with the embezzlement. You've every reason not to let people get close to you. You've every reason to push me away, after what happened when we last…"

Catie closed her eyes, and felt hope die in her. Her father. He'd found out about her father. Not her, not Brazzer, not *Sizzle*. He'd forgiven her for being a helpless victim of fate, not for the shitty choices she'd actually made.

"Captain Seenan sounds thorough," she said.

"I'm still waiting on the full report," Jake said, and took her hand in his. Somehow, he managed a solemn grin. "Anything else I should know?"

Catie laughed, shaking her head to keep herself from crying. Oh, if only. She had a reprieve, nothing more. Captain Seenan was still digging. She met Jake's eyes, and the warm light she saw there tormented her. She knew she should tell him. Right now was the moment to tell him. Right now was the moment to come clean, to confess, to take her chances and throw herself on his mercy, even though she hadn't had a chance to try to fix it yet.

She should do it. She should speak.

Catie opened her mouth, but no sound came out. Suddenly she wondered if Jake was right. Did she do what he said? Did she drive people away, right when they got close to her? Jake had gotten in her head like no one had before, and this was what he had found. He had been inside her, and he'd decided he still liked her. The man had just taught her something about herself, something nobody else had ever been able to do, and he still looked at her as though he loved her.

That was something Catie had never even allowed herself to wish for. That was something she'd thought happened only for other people.

She wasn't strong enough to throw it away.

"No," she said, choking back tears. "There's nothing else."

chapter 25

Jake knew at once that she had lied. Her eyes fluttered, looked briefly away, the silver lilt of her voice with one off note. He had looked inside himself again for the anger he had been sure he would feel as he climbed the stairs to the sound of Catie crying, knowing it came from the library, and was still surprised to find relief in its stead.

He really had felt relief when he saw Catie crying amidst Stephan's letters. Yes, a kind of obligatory shock and anger, but they passed, flashes in the pan. They left behind a cool, flowing sense of release, that finally, finally, someone knew. That finally Catie, in particular, knew. He hadn't had to come up with some torturous way to explain; she'd seen for herself. And if she decided she didn't want to have anything to do with him, well, he wouldn't necessarily blame her.

But just the look on her face had told him he didn't need to be concerned about that. And it had given him the latest in a series of emotions he'd never dreamed he'd be able to feel. Joy. A weird, strange joy, when the woman he loved was crying and the evidence of a tragedy lay about everywhere, but joy, just the same. One more thing he owed to Catie.

It had been quickly supplanted by confusion. She was still hiding something.

"Are you sure?" he asked her.

She nodded, wiping at her eyes. Another lie. He had never been this attuned to another human being. It felt improper, in a strange way, like he was eavesdropping, and at the moment, what he heard hurt him deeply.

Captain Seenan had given only the barest details: her father, poor excuse for a man and a father both, a thief who'd abandoned her; mother dead; etcetera. Only family left was a grandmother in a home somewhere. There were some hints at an outlandish youth, acting out, never getting the attention she needed. Not an uncommon story, but that it was Catie's story made it special to him.

Yet still she hid from him. She was like a wild animal when wounded, determined to hide until she healed. Only Jake was certain that he owed her more than that. Whatever wonderful thing was happening to him, he was certain he owed it to her, and equally certain it would not survive if she left. He wouldn't scare her off.

He reached for her cheek, but she backed away.

"How are you not pissed?" she said again. She

was almost angry now, the way people become angry when they don't understand what's going on and it frightens them. "How are you not, just...freaking out?"

"I don't know," he said honestly. He wouldn't let go of her hand. He had begun to think of it as a lifeline. "I am, in a removed way. But I am also...I am *relieved*. I hid that for so long, worried about what you would think, if you knew. And there are other things, too. Catie, those letters were not wrong. What I told you was true. I was heartless, in a way; not incapable of feeling, but incapable...it is hard to describe. I couldn't bear intimacy of any kind with another human being, least of all the kind where someone in pain depended upon me."

"You used the past tense," she said quietly.

"Yes. You were there with me, in the dining room. You know that doesn't fully describe me anymore, at least where you are concerned."

His own words sounded bloodless to him. 'Doesn't describe me anymore?' Like he was speaking of a passing acquaintance, a casual encounter, rather than the life-changing thing that she had done for him. Jake looked at Catie, wilting in shadows just beyond the range of the light from the desk lamp, and struggled to do better.

"Your false name," he said, and she stiffened again. "You used that for a reason."

Slowly, she nodded.

"You wanted to become someone else? To leave it behind?"

Catie didn't say anything. He badly wanted to touch her, but forced himself to speak. "That's how I feel, in a way. I have become different. Something has happened to me, because of you. I am... *Damn*."

He couldn't say it yet, didn't have any facility for intimate language. Maybe he'd get there eventually, maybe not, but for now, he had to use what he had. He wrapped his arm around her waist and kissed her.

It only seemed to make it worse. He could feel her wilting further, collapsing in upon herself to some far place he couldn't reach. He didn't understand.

"Catie," he said, as she drew away.

"I don't deserve this," she said.

She meant his kindness.

She looked tinier than she ever had, shrunken, as though she were trying to disappear. Jake thought back to the first time he'd brought her into this very room, when he tried to explain what his deficiencies were—deficiencies Catie had somehow begun to heal. He'd tried to explain how he achieved catharsis through domination, how it was the closest he could come to intimacy, how the rules and strictures gave him a kind of freedom.

"Like a sonnet," he said under his breath.

Catie looked at him, and something glimmered in her eye—that spark that he loved so much.

She'd said she needed submission in the same way. That it gave her the same release. Catharsis. And now she was huddled in front of him, so consumed with self-loathing that he couldn't reach her.

Except perhaps one way.

"I think you need to see that no matter how far you push me," he said, "I'm not going anywhere."

He moved forward, and instinctively she moved back, as though they'd already started the dance. In just a few steps she hit the back bookcase, sandwiched between the two large windows. Slowly, deliberately, he reached down to grab her hands, and brought them up over her head.

Catie sucked in her breath and looked up. "Punish me," she said. He looked down the length of her body to see her chest rising and falling rapidly, her stomach fluttering. He knew if he put his hand in her pants, he'd find her wet.

Jake thought back to their first session, remembered her response to pain. To discipline. He slid one hand down her arm to palm her breast, and viciously pinched her nipple.

"Ah," she cried, and her breathing intensified. Her eyes were large, and had become languid, deep. She looked right at him and said, "Yes. Please. *Please.*"

Catie had given him the ability to love. He would give her anything she needed.

"Take off your clothes," he said, releasing her hands. "And bend over that couch."

chapter 26

Catie shivered at the sound of his voice. Authoritative. Demanding. Urgent.

She met his eye, and slowly began to unbutton her blouse. Her awareness of her body — of his eyes on her body — increased with every button.

"Quicker," he said, his voice thick.

She shed her blouse, unzipped her skirt. Soon, her clothing lay in an inert pile at her feet, and she felt the calm start to come over her, the stress and anguish of knowing she'd failed Jake — again — fading into the background.

She started to move towards the couch, but he stopped her.

"Wait," he said. "Spread your legs."

Catie obeyed automatically. It wasn't until she felt his hand push between her legs that she remembered: today was Friday.

She had screwed up.

Before she could speak, his fingers spread her lips and probed her flesh. Jake frowned.

"Today is Friday," he said. "Something is missing."

Catie felt the heat spread through her body and rise to the surface of her skin, where it burned. She was both genuinely ashamed and, somehow, thrilled.

"I forgot, sir."

His finger swirled carelessly, and Catie's eyelids fluttered. He shook his head in slight disappointment. "Beneath the couch there is a box. Retrieve it."

Catie padded across the floor, grateful for the no doubt priceless rugs. She had once felt awkward about being naked, in a strange way, but Jake had since given her a different sense of her own body. Every movement was part of their game, every gesture charged with desire, with the potential for pleasure. She could feel his eyes on her every step of the way.

"Open it."

She did. It held what she expected: various toys, accoutrements, and equipment. She no longer wasted time thinking about what other women might have seen similar things in Jake's presence. For right now, this moment, she knew she was all he thought about.

"This has earned you…more," he said.

She bent her head, and tried not to smile. "Yes, sir."

"Bend over, hands on the couch, as you were

before."

She shuddered. Every movement seemed to occur in slow motion. She bent slowly at the waist, keeping her back rigid and slightly arched, feeling the pull on her hamstrings. She placed first one palm and then the other flat on the rich red leather. And then, with her head down, she thrust her bottom ever so slightly towards him. An offering.

He said nothing. She heard him rustle through the box, heard him take out several items. He must know what the anticipation did to her.

Finally, she felt it. First a swab of lube, his fingers rough and unyielding. Then the cold, round metal of the ben-wa balls.

"This time, you will take it with these inside," he said, removing the metal and pushing one, two fingers inside her, moving them about. "And you will *not* come. Do you understand?"

Catie bit her lip. She already felt dangerously aroused, dangerously alive. The forlorn despair of moments ago was long forgotten. Now an orgasm seemed to lurk just over the horizon.

But she would try.

"Yes, sir," she said.

He didn't hesitate, but pushed the first ball into her quickly, making her eyes pop open and a small sound escape her lips. She felt his hand on her buttocks, gripping the flesh and pulling it wide, and then the second ball pushing in after the first, feeling impossibly large and impossibly wide, simply too much volume to take — until she did.

"Oh God," she heard herself murmur. These were bigger. She felt full, forced to squeeze down to keep them in. Her arms started to shake.

Jake stroked her, up and down, up and down, seemingly just to torment her. "Remember," he said, and she thought she detected a hint of a smile, "you are not to come."

"Yes…sir," she said.

He was gone for a just a moment, and then she felt the first blow. The pain was only slight, quickly blooming into pleasure, and her body lurched forward. The ben-wa balls shook inside her, vibrating rapidly, and her muscles started to contract despite herself.

"Count the strokes," he said.

She shook her head, trying to clear her mind.

"I said, *count them.*"

"One," she gasped.

Just as she'd managed to quell the contractions, he struck her again. She couldn't tell what he was using—a riding crop? It didn't matter. She hung her head, quivering.

"Two," she said softly.

He struck her again, a long, broad stroke across her most sensitive flesh. She cried out as the spring in the balls rattled, vibrating inside her.

"Do *not* come," he repeated.

She breathed in, out. Her whole body wanted to contract in one, giant orgasm. That he forbade it brought it that much closer to fruition. She gritted her teeth.

"Yes, sir. I'll do my best, sir."

There was a pause. Then he struck her again, lightly, and again, harder, and then again, leaving no room to breathe, no time to collect herself, no opportunity for recovery.

She almost made it.

She came, the orgasm tearing out of her throat in a long cry. He held her hips as she did so, held her up while her head sank to the red leather below. He must have known what he was doing to her, must have known what would happen. The backs of her thighs still stung in a delicious way and her legs still quivered, and every contraction brought forth more vibration from the ben-wa balls.

"Jake," she wailed into the couch. His hand smoothed over her buttock in response.

He waited. She didn't know how long, but it was just as she came to, held up pathetically by his hands, her bottom still in the air.

"I told you not to come," he said.

"You knew I would," she panted.

She thought she heard him chuckle.

"But not enough," he said. She turned her head as she felt him pull, again, on the string connecting the ben-wa balls. As it had been at the bar, the tugs against her flesh from the inside sent shivering shocks through her body and her knees buckled. He pulled them out, first one, then the other, and each one leveled her.

Jake ran his hand from her buttock to her hip and up the side of her body, taking his time and giving her some opportunity to recover so that she was fully aware when he cupped her left breast in his large hand. He squeezed, kneading the nipple, and spread her with his other hand.

"You come with me inside you," he said, and plunged into her.

Catie arched her back and her hips followed their natural movement, trying to take as much of him as she could. His thrusts were rapid, and she came again almost instantly, too fast, short, fast little contractions that still left her unsatisfied. Jake slapped her on the side of her ass, telling her, "Not yet."

When he pulled out, she groaned. Her body felt a wreck; she needed completion. He hauled her up, her body not quite boneless, not quite strong, and spun her around. Before she knew what was happening, his hands were back down on her butt, lifting her up, her legs wrapping around him. He supported her completely, and she collapsed around his neck. Slowly he lowered her down, spearing her onto his still erect cock. She moaned as the length of it slid into her. He still held her up by his hands, her full weight pressing into his fingers, his fingers digging deep into the soft flesh. He lifted her slightly, bent his knees, and thrust upwards, hard.

She screamed into his neck and bit down.

She felt his whole body tense, and he thrust into her again, harder, longer. As quickly as he could, he walked out of the library, still inside her, down the hall, until she heard him open a door.

Catie looked up. His bedroom.

His bed.

He fucked her upright all the way to his bed, not at all bothered by her weight, by the strain, by the sheer athletic demand. She was helpless in his arms as he drove into her, again and again, and as they fell down on the bed, all she wanted, strangely, was to drown in him, to be completely full of him until she had no room for the other things that crowded her troubled mind.

He obliged.

chapter 27

They slept together, if you could call it sleeping. Jake woke her twice to make love, once with the brittle winter light streaming through the windows, hitting his face as it had the night before as he slung her leg over his shoulder and gently rocked her to another orgasm. She should have slept like a rock after all that, but the time between, with his naked limbs wrapped behind her, was anything but restful; the contact between them was like a constant buzz, an incessant droning that built and built until it would wake one of them and they'd need each other again.

Catie eventually slept, she supposed, when Jake left. When she woke, the room was dark; he'd drawn the drapes against the light for her. It took her a moment to get her bearings.

She forgot to feel guilty for one or two blissful minutes. And then it all came back.

Catie shot out of bed. She had to find Jake.

She *had* to fix this.

Catie ran to get something to wear, wrapped in nothing but a sheet, and stole a glance at clock. She stopped, stared at it. *Holy shit, it's four o'clock in the afternoon*. She'd slept all damn day. The auction—the *auction*—was at eight.

And where the hell was Jake?

Catie forced herself to slow down and think. She walked back to Jake's bed and sat, rewrapping the sheet around her for her comfort. She hadn't had the courage to tell him the truth last night, not when looking him right in the eye, knowing she'd actually *see* him lose faith in her. But that gnawing worry that ate away at her—*that* was the realization that she couldn't bring herself to stand up at the auction and let Jake bid on her, either. Maybe it was silly to think that *that*, of all things, was going too far, but Catie had gotten accustomed to thinking of herself as a liar, and Jake as the man she lied to. She hadn't accepted the idea that she'd make a fool of him, too.

And where was he, anyway? The auction was in four hours, and Catie had assumed he would take her. Yet she'd avoided talking about it, she realized, in the same way she'd avoided talking about other things that reminded her of her guilt. Still, it wasn't like Jake to just leave her with no explanation.

Catie walked back to the library to retrieve her phone. It was there, battery dying. No messages. She was about to call Jake when she realized what *wasn't* there: the book he'd left her. *Crossing the Rubicon.*

She found it next to the bed. Jake's bed. With a note stuck between the pages, hanging out at a jaunty angle. He'd left it there for her all along.

I had obligations at the charity, and thought you could use the sleep. I've promised dinner with Eileen Corrigan, but will meet you at the auction.

And then, a telltale hesitation mark, just before he signed—

Love, J.

It had taken a lot for him to write that word, "love." But he'd done it.

Catie told herself that she would not cry. She was no longer going to just feel terrible about doing terrible things; Jake deserved better than that. She had to *do* something, she just didn't know what. The book itself felt heavy in her hands, and she found herself wondering about what he'd told her: that she pushed people away by crossing boundaries. She knew it was true. In fact she knew, holding that book, thinking about her life and all the people in it, that it went deeper than that. She was so convinced she'd never be able to rely on anyone, so sure that faith would always be betrayed, that she had to make it come true before anyone had a chance to hurt her. So she just crisscrossed various Rubicons, burning the bridges behind her, left and right. And if she failed to fix this thing with Brazzer, that would be a Rubicon, all right. And if she were being honest, she knew she had already crossed one with Jake. She loved him, beyond all repair. There was no going back.

She read the note again. He was going to dinner with Eileen? Eileen, who'd written him that horrible letter, who'd blamed him for her son's suicide? Catie thought back; the letters had been dated around this time of the year. Just a few days after Valentine's Day, actually.

Oh God. Was this the anniversary?

He was going to dinner with Eileen Corrigan on the anniversary of Stephan's suicide.

Catie had spent her life convinced that people were faithless and not to be relied upon, and yet, here was Jake, making sure he was there for Eileen Corrigan, no matter how much pain they'd brought each other in the past. On a day Catie was sure he would have preferred to be holed up somewhere, keeping his grief to himself, Jake was instead making sure that he was there for everyone else: Eileen, Volare, Catie.

If Jake could be faithful, so could Catie. She could be worthy of…well, no, she couldn't. She'd already screwed up too badly. She had already chickened out the previous night, and the thought of it filled her with bitter shame. What could she do, but confess and alert them to the impending story, to Brazzer's other source? She so wanted to be able to tell them she'd fixed it, that she'd found the source, before she had to reveal what she herself had done — or almost done. But she couldn't even get to Jake before the auction.

"What the hell am I going to do?" she said, quietly, in a very empty room.

Her phone answered her. It buzzed an alert: one new message.

> Last chance. Going to press with what
> we got. - Brazzer

She had run out of time.

chapter 28

Jake smiled encouragingly across the table at Eileen. He would have guessed he'd see Manhattan besieged by swarms of flying pigs, fighting it out in doomed air battles with the pigeons, before he'd see Eileen Corrigan nervous.

Eileen took another sip of her wine and managed a fleeting smile back.

Jake had still had trepidations about this dinner—an entire meal predicated on sharing intimate moments of grief and mourning seemed like exactly the sort of thing he would fail miserably at—but he was finding that whatever new skills or sensitivities he'd developed because of Catie transferred at least moderately well to other situations. He didn't want to get up and run, for example. He thought he was doing rather well.

Eileen, on the other hand, normally the center of any room or conversation, seemed unable to speak. In the lulls, Jake inevitably thought back to Catie; he felt terrible about leaving her in the house after that night—and morning—but he couldn't bring himself to wake her. He hadn't much practice with that sort of thing. Then he'd realize he was thinking about Catie, naked, in his bed, while at what amounted to a memorial dinner, and he'd feel terrible all over again.

Conversation had stalled.

Jake decided to try the direct route. "Eileen, did you have something...in particular that you wanted to tell me?" he said gently. She'd said a lot over the years, in various ways. Whatever it was, Jake could take it. He steeled himself.

"Oh, Jesus, Mary, and Joseph, I don't know why this is so hard," Eileen said, and grabbed her purse from the floor, where she'd insisted on keeping it. She opened it and started to root around. Jake guessed it was so she wouldn't have to look at him. She went on, "You know what was easy? Yelling at you. Saying awful things to you, things I knew weren't true even at the time. The worst things I could think of—that was easy. Saying something *nice*—that's hard."

Jake said, "What—?"

"Oh, shut up, Jake, let me get it out. I'm on a roll now, I might never do it otherwise."

Eileen fetched a pile of papers from her bottomless beige bag and put them on the table between the bread rolls and the olive oil. It was a jumble—folded sheets of typed pages, longhand on fancy stationary, even scraps. Jake recognized the handwriting on a few visible pieces. Stephan.

It just sat there, sucking up all the sound in the room.

"What's this?" he asked. He was unable to take his eyes off the papers. He noticed that she'd tied them together with butcher's string.

"This is the stuff of his I found afterwards that I never told you about," Eileen said. She took a deep breath. "Jake, you have to understand, I was so *angry*. So, so angry. I felt like I never even had a chance with him, he'd cut me out so early. But now, I don't know…"

Eileen trailed off, and when Jake looked up she was wiping one eye delicately with her finger. Her mascara hadn't run.

"Well," she said. "The upshot is that most of those things mention you. There's a hodgepodge journal, some of his short stories, odds and ends. Poems and stuff. You know he wasn't organized. But he loved you. He admired you in so many ways, and he wrote about the things you gave him, spending time with him, especially after Harry died."

Jake and Stephan had felt like they only had each other after their dad died, leaving out Eileen in that self-centered way of adolescents. And then Jake hadn't been there on that one particular night. Jake could feel the failure all over again, just as fresh as if it had been last week. Apparently now he wore his pain on his face, because Eileen reached across and grabbed his hand.

"Hey! Listen to me. I'm not saying that you screwed up; I'm saying you were a good thing in his life. I'm saying you made it better. I'm saying that what I wrote to you…I was wrong. Do you hear me? I was *wrong*."

Jake finally looked her in the eye. She looked furious in an oddly motherly sort of way, her green eyes glaring at him with the same intensity he could remember when he and Stephan would get into trouble as kids.

"You *listen* to me, Jacob Jayson," she said. "I was wrong. I was angry, and looking for someone to blame because I was sure that I…" She caught herself, shook her head slightly, and plowed ahead. "It was no one's fault. Stephan was sick. We all did the best we could. I asked you here to tell you that and to give you these so you could see for yourself how you did good by him. Ok?"

Bewildered, Jake didn't know what else to say. He said, "Ok."

Eileen squeezed his hand. "Then what are you waiting for?" she said, looking at the pile of papers. "Take 'em, they're not going to burn you."

Gingerly, Jake reached for them. She was right— they didn't burn. He'd have all the time in the world to read them, though he wasn't sure he wanted to. No, he did want to. He just…

"While I'm on the subject," Eileen said, taking up her wine glass again and swirling it with a little too much deliberation, "I'm also sorry for giving you the cold shoulder when you were a boy. Harry might've had a wandering eye before we got married, but that was no reason to take it out on you."

Eileen had now broached the two areas of conversation Jake had never expected to hear anyone speak of out loud in real life. He looked around in confusion, as though expecting to find evidence of a hallucination or a perverse candid camera show.

"Aren't you going to say anything?" she asked.

"I think I'm a little overwhelmed," he said honestly.

"Yeah, well, I'm not done yet," Eileen grinned. "What the hell are you doing with that girl Catie?"

Jake felt a little as though he had only just learned to walk, in the sense of being able to relate to people in a somewhat normal way without shutting down, and Eileen had taken the opportunity to demand that he run the four hundred meter hurdles competitively. All he could think of was what he had done with Catie that morning.

He swallowed uncomfortably. "Eileen, I'm not sure that's appropriate—"

"Oh, for Chrissakes, not *that*," she said, leaning across the table to swat his arm and looking, to Jake's relief, genuinely annoyed. Annoyance he could deal with. "Listen, your mother…was your mother, and obviously she did kind of a number on you, and then I'm sure I didn't help when I threw you a nasty curveball. But I've been watching you the past couple of weeks, and I've been asking around, and I can tell, Jakey, you've been punishing yourself. You're determined to be alone and solitary and all that crap, like the Beast in that movie—you remember that? You boys loved that Disney movie, made me promise not to tell anyone because it was a girls' movie." Eileen laughed, looked for a cigarette, and seemed to frown when she remembered they were in a restaurant. "You remember how you cried?"

Jake had a memory of hiding his face in the theater, seated between his dad and his brother, Eileen on the end, and thinking he'd done a good job of it. "No, actually," he lied.

"Well, you did. Loved that goddamn movie. But you're not a hideous beast, you dummy, and I can tell you have a shot with that girl, and you deserve a chance. If that's the best I can do for you, I'm gonna make sure you have a chance."

She worried him with the determination so clearly evident in her face. Eileen Corrigan was a woman who lived her life as a series of missions. Jake was having the slow epiphany that he'd become one of those missions.

"What?" he said. "How?"

"You heard me. You still screwing that up with that girl Catie?" Eileen narrowed her eyes. "Tell me the truth."

"No," he said. "No, I don't think so."

"You sure about that?"

Jake shrugged helplessly. He was new to all this, after all. For all he knew, he might be screwing up at this very moment.

"Yeah, well," Eileen said, finally going for a piece of bread, "I got something I want to say to her, too. You were taking her to that charity thing tonight, right? I'm gonna tag along so I can have a word with her."

Jake gripped the table with both hands. Now that Eileen had gotten the hardest, most heartfelt things off her chest, she had reverted with remarkable ease to her old self. He was having trouble adjusting at the same rate, but one thing he was certain of: he did *not* want Eileen Corrigan anywhere near a Volare event, not even one that was conducted with discretion.

"I'm not sure that's a good idea," he finally said.

"Don't be silly," Eileen grabbed another piece of bread. "I won't even go inside, I'll be out of your hair like that, don't worry. But I *am* going to speak to her," she finished, jabbing the bread in the air pointedly. "Tonight."

Jake sat quietly for a long time, making only polite conversation while their dinner came and went, trying to work out what reaction he was having to everything Eileen had said. His mind had shut out any attempt to contemplate the papers and things she'd brought about Stephan—that was far too big for him to deal with over dinner. Instead he focused on his mild horror at the idea of Eileen coming to speak to Catie, at his discomfort, and, most importantly, at his apparent acceptance that this was something that was sane. He didn't like it, but it didn't seem outlandish, or like a crisis. Watching and listening to Eileen gossip about the women who worked at Stephan's House and the people back in Eileen's neighborhood, people he hadn't seen in years, Jake finally realized that this was the closest thing to a mother that he'd ever had.

Maybe he should listen to her.

chapter 29

Catie did not know what to do. That in and of itself
was not unusual; she was almost getting used to
that particular feeling. But right now, at this
moment, it kind of mattered. She had arrived, as
Jake had instructed her to, at the site of the Volare
Valentine's Auction—which, he'd neglected to
mention, was actually outdoors, in heated tents set
up in a sort of winter wonderland of the Frick
Museum Gardens—but she could not find Jake.
And Catie had no intention of going up there and
letting him bid on her without coming clean. She
just couldn't do it. Maybe it was a stupid line to
draw after all the crap she'd pulled, but it was her
line in the sand. The last, final Rubicon, and this
one…well, the metaphor kind of broke down there,
she reflected. But it was one last thing she couldn't

do.

She'd come here with the intention of first telling Jake, then telling Roman, or letting him tell Roman, or something, then trying to find a way to help them mitigate the effects of what she'd done, and what Brazzer was about to do. Or offer herself up for ritual sacrifice, whatever. She grimly refused to think about the worst-case scenario, which was that she would be unable to help in any way, and none of them would ever want to see or speak to her ever again.

Which was that, above all, she would lose Jake.

Some crazy part of her held on to the hope that she wouldn't lose him, even though she knew she deserved to. She figured that hope was the only reason she'd be able to actually go through with it.

But her plan, she realized now, as she walked in and out of the well-appointed museum rooms set aside for prep and reception of the auction, depended utterly on being able to find both Jake *and* Roman. Or at least one of them.

She didn't even see Lola. Where the hell was everyone? Was there some secret room where they were all planning things? How was it possible she couldn't find anyone amidst a sea of beautiful people? That was the thing about this crowd — Lola had joked about little old ladies, and maybe that's what it had been in the beginning when the tradition got started, but it looked like all the non-Volare people had come here right from Fashion Week. Catie wondered what they'd all been told about the event.

But even if Catie couldn't find anyone, that didn't mean she couldn't be found. Someone grabbed her shoulder, and she jumped about a foot.

"Whoa," Courtney said. Catie was momentarily relieved. Courtney, at least, was a friendly face, one of the people who'd made her feel at home when she'd first come to Volare. Catie thought of her as a friend. Well, until word of her deceit got around. Then she'd probably be another person Catie would miss.

"What's up," Catie said, forcing a smile. "Listen, have you seen Jake? I really, *really* need to find him."

"Nope. Thought he'd be with you. But there is someone who says she needs to speak to you," Courtney said, reaching across to steal a bacon-wrapped candied date from a passing tray. "Red-haired lady, waiting for you in the room with all the sculpture busts."

Red-haired lady? Eileen!

"You ok?" Courtney asked. The look of genuine concern on her face gave Catie another pang of guilt.

"Yeah, I'm just..." Catie couldn't finish. She couldn't think of a good reason why Eileen Corrigan would need to see her right now. In fact, she couldn't think of any reasons at all that weren't disastrous. "Which direction are the heads in?"

Courtney pointed, and Catie flew off without an explanation. She knew it was rude, but odds were that Courtney would think much worse of her before the night was over. And she couldn't shake the feeling that something was wrong with Jake.

Eileen was, indeed, waiting amidst the sculpture heads, looking critically at a bust of Pompey. She looked up when Catie rushed into the room and raised her eyebrows at Catie's dress.

Catie had found it at Jake's. He'd apparently had it made for her for this very event, and it was…well, it was flattering, definitely. Whether it was more for the benefit of Catie or Jake was up for debate. Catie would have called it nearly see-through, except she was sure it was by a very expensive designer, and thus probably should be called "sheer."

"That is some dress," Eileen said. "You sure that's right for a charity auction?"

"Um."

"Maybe it's just the light in here," Eileen said, eyebrows still up.

"I think so," Catie said. She looked around, somehow disappointed not to find Jake. "Eileen, is everything ok? Jake was supposed to meet me here, but I can't find him."

"Yeah, that's 'cause I told him I wanted to talk to you," Eileen said. She was still looking at the Roman bust. "Did all these guys really look alike?"

"Eileen," Catie said. The older woman looked at her with a sense of satisfaction. Catie was still baffled; she felt like a nervous wreck. "I really need to find him. What did you want to say to me?"

"First, you need to relax," Eileen said, taking her arm. "Trust me, I'm older than you. No good comes out of panicking. Second…" She stopped and turned to look Catie in the eye. Catie hadn't noticed how short Eileen was; the woman had always seemed large by sheer force of personality. Right now, though, it seemed like she needed to ask something of Catie, and that made her look smaller.

"I need you to do me a favor," she said gravely.

"Anything, Eileen, but just please tell me where he is. Is he out talking to the crowd?" Catie hadn't checked among the people gathered in the heated tents because she didn't recognize most of them and she thought he'd be backstage with Volare. Now she was convinced she'd missed him.

"What?" Eileen scoffed. "Oh God, no — after his media whore mother, he hates that kind of thing. Publicity and crowds and glad-handing and all that makes him sick, he'll be skulking in the shadows somewhere or something."

Catie felt a large lump form in her throat. *Publicity makes him sick. Media whore mother.* She had been totally deluded to think there was ever a chance he would forgive her for giving any information at all to Brazzer, for planning to sell him out to *Sizzle,* even if she hadn't pulled the trigger. How could he? She'd lied to him all this time, and she'd done it for the worst reason.

"Listen to me," Eileen went on. "This is important, ok? I need you to give him a break. Cut him some slack. He's a good man who's had a rougher time than you know, and so he's, you know, a little rough around the edges, is all. I just want you to promise me you'll be gentle with him, let him mess up a little bit. He means well."

Catie couldn't believe what she was hearing. She found she couldn't meet the other woman's eye anymore, so she took her hand. "Eileen, I can promise you that I will do my best."

"Good. This might not seem like such a big deal to you, I know, but trust me. I owe him, which means it's important to me, too." Eileen fixed her with what Catie guessed was supposed to be an intimidating glare. If only Eileen knew. Instead she seemed placated, and chucked Catie under the chin affectionately.

"He's got all that money," Eileen said softly. "But not too many people have done right by him. You do what you can, that's all I'm saying."

Catie closed her eyes. She had tears welling up behind her eyelids. If she opened them, it would be all over.

"You're sure you don't know where he is?" she said.

"No, and he made me promise not to stay here, for some reason," Eileen said dubiously. "You ok?"

"I'm fine, just hay fever. Eileen, thank you, but I have to run," Catie said, turning away and hurrying toward the exit. From behind, she heard Eileen call out.

"It's February!"

But Catie kept running until she found a bathroom. The tears had started, and she had to let them pass. She knew she only had a few minutes. She thought of them as the last minutes before her world, such as it was, such as she'd been able to build in a short time in a strange city, was about to come apart. If she hadn't been certain that she didn't deserve one iota of Jake's forgiveness before, what Eileen said had sealed it. She had to be honest with herself: the hope she'd been holding on to was most likely a lost cause.

That didn't change the fact that she should still do the right thing. And it didn't change the fact that she knew she should think better of Jake. Jake, of all people—Jake, who could find a way to be there for Eileen Corrigan—Jake deserved better. If she was ever going to put her faith in anyone, now was the time. Jake was the man.

Catie wiped her eyes, and made a decision.

chapter 30

"Forgive my rudeness, Roman," Jake said as soon as he closed the door, "but please, spit it out. You have no idea the day I've already had."

Roman had taken his arm almost as soon as Jake had entered the building, leaving Eileen to find Catie on her own. Jake had protested; Roman had said there was something important they needed to talk about. That was about the last thing Jake had wanted to hear. The previous night with Catie and then dinner with Eileen had used up his important talk quota for a long, long time. Didn't everyone know he wasn't any good at this? Only now, because of Catie, was he getting slightly better.

He felt like a prizefighter on the wrong end of twelve rounds.

But Roman never looked worried, and

now…well, Roman looked worried. So Jake had followed him to what was, apparently, a coatroom.

"Don't keep me in suspense, Roman," he said.

"Are you nervous?" Roman asked him.

"What? Why should I be nervous? When have you ever known me to be nervous?"

Jake himself could name a few instances in recent memory, but he decided not to mention recent events. Roman, however, absolutely looked…distressed. His old friend took a deep breath and frowned.

"Where is Catie?" Roman said.

"I don't know, Roman, we arrived separately. I had another engagement for dinner."

"Did she tell you anything? Anything important?"

Jake threw up his hands. "Roman, for the last time—what the hell are you talking about?"

Roman himself looked like he was in unfamiliar territory. Jake had a hard time puzzling it out, but eventually it hit him: Roman looked like a man who was dealing with failure.

Finally Roman looked up, his face a mask of sorrow. "I was so sure," he said.

Before Jake could throttle his friend in frustration, there was a knock at the door. This in and of itself was odd—it was a coat room, not an office—but they didn't have to wait long. The door opened, and Vincent Duran slipped in and closed the door behind him.

"This is a farce, isn't it?" Jake said. He sat down on a pile of coats, and decided to wait, as patiently as possible, until everyone else regained their minds. Or until he had to go bid on Catie. He had planned to surface just long enough to claim his woman — he smiled at the thought — then get them both out of there and back to his bedroom as soon as possible. He was determined that nothing would interfere with that part of his plan.

"Lola told me you were in here," Vincent said. "Sorry, man, but this could *not* wait — trust me."

Vincent looked uncomfortably at Jake.

"Uh, Roman, it's about the…situation."

Jake looked up at the ceiling. "Is someone going to tell me what the hell is going on?"

"He should hear it now, too," Roman said quietly.

Vincent wasted no time. "She's been working for fucking *Sizzle*," he spat. "They're doing a big, glossy feature! Somehow they got photos! A goddamn *photo spread*."

"Based on her reporting?" Roman asked quickly. "How do you know?"

"Wait a minute," Jake said.

Vincent ran his hand through his hair, agitated. "I went out with a girl in their finance department a few times in L.A., called in a favor after Lola got me her real name — which, by the way, bro, Lola is fucking *pissed* at you," he gave Roman a pitying look. "Anyway, had my girl check the tax records. BAM. Paid in small dippy amounts for probably little stories, but she's on the rolls, man. There's no way she's not his source."

"Not necessarily," Roman said. "In fact, not even probably, if the focus is on the glossy spread. At least it is not *only* her."

While Jake listened to this, he had begun to feel very strange. He felt slightly queasy, like he had once as a teenager the morning after he'd first tried tequila, and there was a pins and needles sensation racing up his back, increasing in intensity. It was not at all pleasant. He got up to pace, just for the movement, his eyes darting about for some target, he didn't know for what purpose.

He wanted to demand an explanation again, but his mouth felt very dry, and he was already dreading what the answer would be.

"What are you talking about?" Vincent asked Roman.

"They already had information for what you would call a drive-by piece, and they already had my name," Roman said. He sounded tired. "So I did what you would have told me to do, Vincent. I took charge of the story. How would you put it? I gave it a spin, to protect the rest of the club. I am the source for *Sizzle*. As part of the agreement, no one else is to be named, so long as they don't have another source. And so long as Brazzer honors it."

"And you *knew* what she was doing?"

"Yes, for the most part," Roman said. As he spoke, he looked steadily at Jake. "I ran the background check, and I found the name of an old friend. Irina had been her acting coach for a time, and Irina loved her. She is a good judge of character, Irina. She told me all about her. I thought we could help her here. I thought Jake would help her. I thought she would make the right choice."

Jake whispered, but his voice was very clear, in the silence that followed.

"Who?" he said, but he already knew.

Roman looked at him very sadly. "Catie."

chapter 31

Snow had begun to fall slowly around the heated tent in the middle of the Frick Gardens, hidden by a high fence from the traffic on Fifth Avenue. The champagne flowed, various red and white lights sparkled in the early February night, the auction was underway, and Catie still hadn't found Jake. She stood like a despairing island amidst a sea of joyous, drunken, slightly debauched fun, shivering even though she wasn't cold. She was certainly running out of time. Nearly out, in fact. As the minutes ticked by, Catie had made contingency plan after contingency plan, but as the auctioneer raced through the catalog, she was down to one: her confession would have to be public.

Catie shivered again.

Worse, she realized that this was probably how

it should have been all along. She didn't owe just Jake an apology, though she owed him most of all; she owed every single person she'd met under false pretenses an apology. She owed everyone who'd shown her kindness while she'd lied to them an apology. She had been dreading this, but it was undeniably right. And she simply couldn't go up there and allow Jake to bid on her.

She'd just have to be creative with her phrasing.

Catie thought about her grandmother and winced. She didn't actually have a back up plan. She had some money put away, and she thought she would be able to beg and plead for a little bit of time, but she would have to think of something soon. Something she could live with this time. It was another leap of faith.

"Next up, we have a spa package at Renopo," Gwen said into the microphone. Catie recognized that item—it was a Volare lot, for sure, one of the subs being auctioned off for a weekend. Nobody had told Catie how the bidding worked; she assumed some of it was prearranged, like her lot was supposed to be, but if the look on a nearby woman's face was any indication, not all of them were. The woman kept biting her lip to keep from smiling, but it wasn't working.

But Catie wasn't overly concerned with that. She was concerned that she was up next.

Her attention wandered to the crowd, trying, one last time, to find Jake. If he were to bid, he'd be out there, surely? But she couldn't find him. The auction had begun to descend into a kind of well-heeled chaos, with various paid performers circulating amongst the party goers, juggling and doing things that required a kind of flexibility that would be highly valued at Volare itself, and society fixtures making drunken passes at models who spoke no English, or pretended not to. Someone she recognized from Volare was drinking vodka as it poured off a delicately carved ice statue. The sub to her right was auctioned off to enthusiastic cheers, and Catie wondered, again, whether any of these people really didn't know what was up. If she had to guess, she'd say they were all in on it; it was just one of those traditions that morphed over the years and became something else entirely.

But she was only wondering about things like that to keep her mind off of what she was about to do, and the inevitable consequences.

She was out of time.

"Next, we have a gourmet dinner of one," Gwen read, and laughed. It was getting to be that part of the evening. "Sorry, *for* one. For two?"

That was Catie's cue. In fact, that was *Catie*, but it was her chance to make it right. Right-ish. Now or never, basically. She stepped up and tapped Gwen on the shoulder.

"Hey, I have something I need to say," she whispered.

Gwen started and turned around wildly, her hand covering the mic.

"Are you canceling the lot?" Gwen asked, wide-eyed. "I can do that for you if you need me to— don't worry. Are you ok?"

Oh man. Another person being nice to her. As if the universe wanted to make absolutely sure she knew what an asshole she'd been.

Catie took a deep breath. "I'm fine. It's not that.

Just…give me the mic."

She stood up before the crowd and took one last look around for Jake. Nothing. The attention of the crowd was scattered, festive, happy. The lots had been auctioned off so far while people enjoyed themselves. All that was about to come to an end.

"Excuse me," Catie said, and tapped the mic. "I have a confession to make."

~ ~ ~

Jake ran through the uncovered part of the gardens, soft, heavy flakes of snow falling all around, lit up from below as they fell, and wished he had time to enjoy the spectacle. He'd spent too much time in the coatroom, thinking. He hadn't even had to think that hard, but he'd been so surprised at how easy his decision was that he'd sort of been taken aback. Eventually he'd checked his watch, and opted for a shortcut through the snow rather than the long way around through the museum itself.

He elbowed his way through the edge of the crowd, looking for Catie. She didn't know she'd been found out, and he didn't want anyone else to be the one to tell her. Vincent was still angry, as was Lola, apparently, and he didn't want them to be the first people she encountered. No one else would understand like he did.

He was almost happy to tell her. Not to tell her the part about her being discovered as a mole or a source or whatever it was you called what she'd planned to do, but the next part. The part about how he felt. The part about how he still loved her anyway.

That's what he'd spent all that time doing in the coatroom. Musing. Marveling at the bare fact of it. He didn't understand it, not in an intellectual sense. In fact, it didn't fully make sense. He should be angry, and he was, but the anger was dwarfed by everything else. Jake finally understood what had happened with Catie the night before, finally understood what had made her cry, finally understood why she'd felt so terrible about herself. And in fact there might not be anyone more equipped to simply understand her plight than him. He, more than anyone else he knew, knew what it was to make a terrible mistake and have to live with it. He couldn't condemn her for it, not when she'd already absolved him of his own inadequacies.

But most of all, even with how bad it looked to someone like Roman—and Jake knew, as Roman could not, that it wasn't as bad as it looked, that Catie wasn't cold and calculating, that she was in fact quite tortured about the whole thing, and the failing health of her grandmother must have weighed on her enormously—most of all, he found that his love for Catie simply just *was*. Perhaps that was a burden as well as a blessing, but for the moment, Jake could only revel in the fact that it was apparently possible for him. He'd said that to people for years, never realizing that he'd unconsciously refused to apply it to love. He'd always meant attraction, or sexuality, or any of the other things he felt he had an understanding of.

But this? This was a revelation. He could love someone *no matter what*. Or, perhaps importantly, he could love *her* no matter what. He couldn't wait to tell her. He couldn't wait to tell the whole world.

But first, he had to find her.

He was searching, in vain, near a melting nude ice sculpture, when instead of seeing her face, he heard her voice.

"Excuse me," she said. "I have a confession to make."

Jake whipped around. He'd never, ever heard her sound frightened like that. Catie stood up at the lectern, her face pale and drawn, waiting for the crowd to quiet down, waiting for all eyes to fall on her. And Jake knew what she was about to do.

"Oh, damn," he said. And started to fight his way through the crowd.

~ ~ ~

Catie had originally pictured herself making a graceful admission of guilt, something eloquent, sincere, heartfelt. Now that the moment was here and she was starting to sweat, she lowered her expectations. Now she was just hoping to make it through without throwing up.

She looked up at the crowd, and then immediately thought better of it. Nope. That was not going to help.

Just put your head down and do it.

"Ok, so," she started, already feeling like a dumb valley girl, "I'll make this short and sweet. Um, not sweet. It's actually the opposite of sweet. But I can't let anyone…" She braved a look up, hoping to catch Jake. Nothing. "I can't let anyone bid on my, uh, dinner, without first coming clean about what I've done. I have not told the truth. Um, actually, I just straight up lied. It's not like I forgot to tell the truth, I just lied. Roberts isn't my real last name. It's Rose. And as I was…getting to know many of you," she went on, totally at a loss for an appropriate euphemism, "you know, in the *organization*, I was also…oh, crap, there's just no good way to say this. I was also looking for material. For a story."

She closed her eyes.

"For *Sizzle*."

That did it. She heard a few gasps, and then the silence slowly became complete, as people in the know or people who were still sober enough to pay attention shushed anyone still chatting innocently. Even people who weren't in Volare among this crowd would know this was a big deal. Famous people, rich people, people in entertainment and fashion, people in politics — none of them liked hearing the word '*Sizzle*.' Catie was pretty sure a few of them were looking over their shoulders.

"It's a story I'm never going to write," she said, her shoulders sinking as she began to relax. It was done. She wasn't anxious any longer, just sad. And she deserved to be pretty sad. "But I'm afraid someone will probably write it. I just wanted to say how sorry I am, and that all of you deserved much better. I've never felt as welcome anywhere — "

Nope. Now she was going to start crying. She had *promised* herself that she would not cry; she had promised herself that she would not make this about her. Nobody ever wants to yell at a crying woman, and they should all feel perfectly free to say whatever they wanted.

"Oh, shit," she said, wiping at her eyes. "I'm just sorry. Really, really sorry."

And then Catie forced herself to look up and face what she'd done. She figured she owed them all at least that. If they wanted to demand answers, ask questions, or pelt her with snowballs, she would take it. Or if they had security kick her the hell out, that would work, too.

But it was worse than any of that. It was just silence. She searched the crowd for the faces she recognized, hoping to see something there, some reaction, some emotion. Anything was better than a vacuum. She saw Lola, looking hurt and furious. She saw Roman, who was, incredibly, smiling. The rest was a sea of anger and confusion, of people who alternately hated her and pitied her, just one after the other. Catie thought she felt bad enough. Looking at those faces, she understood she should feel even worse.

But she didn't see the one face, in the end, who mattered.

She gripped the lectern, not wanting to turn away until she'd seen him, until she'd at least seen, for herself, that he hated her, or was disgusted, or anything really, anything at all except not knowing. But again, she had to face facts: she didn't deserve to ask anything of him. If he wanted to never see her again, to never be in her presence, to pretend as though she didn't exist...

Catie started to shake. She was about to lose it.

"Ok," she said, nodding. "Ok, that was it."

She turned, about to give the lectern back to a stunned Gwen, when she heard him.

"Hey!"

Catie froze, not quite willing to believe her luck. She still couldn't see him. The voice came from somewhere in the back of the crowd, where people were starting to clear away.

"Is that lot still up? Lot twenty-three?"

Catie felt the beginnings of a smile. Just the sound of his voice…but it was more than that. The way she could tell he was smiling, just by his tone. The way he sounded like…he was teasing her?

She had wanted, more than anything, to get down and out of the spotlight, to go hide somewhere where she could be alone with her shame and her wretchedness—or whatever it was people were supposed to feel in these situations. She was open to the pillory or the stocks, even. All those angry faces looking out at her had only compounded her guilt, magnifying every instance of shame, making her relive all of her offenses one by one. And even though she felt like she deserved it, that didn't mean she was strong enough to take it, at least not for very long.

But his voice…

She could stay up there all night now. She would, if he wanted her to. *Just let me see him.*

Gwen gently took the mic and angled it toward her while Catie searched the crowd.

"I think so? Lot twenty-three?" Gwen said. She looked at Catie, then at Roman, then back to Catie. Catie wasn't even paying attention. "Let's go with yes on Lot twenty-three. If we have any bidders?"

That was an open question.

"You do."

Jake stepped out from behind a melting ice sculpture, his hand up in the air. He was smiling.

He was looking at her with those dark, shining eyes, and he was *smiling*. Why would he be smiling after what she'd just said? Why would he be putting his hand up in the air? Why—?

"What's your bid, sir?" Gwen said into the microphone.

Jake walked toward the lectern, his eyes locked on Catie. She was struck by one of those superstitious compulsions again, where she dared not move for fear of jinxing whatever the hell was happening.

He mounted the stone steps, taking Catie in hand, his arm around her waist. She didn't understand. She didn't believe this was happening. Even as he leaned in to whisper in her ear, she couldn't quite believe it.

Not until he said, "Everybody makes mistakes. I still love you."

"You love me?" Catie said as he brushed a tear off her cheek.

Jake shrugged, still smiling like he'd just made an amazing discovery. "Some things just *are*," he said. Then he leaned in to the mic. "I bid everything. All of it. Whatever it takes."

Roman himself started the applause.

epilogue

Catie watched her friend Danny Boylan, recently back from his theatrical tour, try to explain to Eileen Corrigan that stage left was not the direction she thought it was, and smiled. The two of them had shown a strange but strong affinity for each other as soon as they'd both started working to develop a theatrical therapy program for Stephan's House, and had driven each other happily insane since. Danny didn't have a great relationship with his family, who weren't overly thrilled with the gay thing, and it filled Catie with a warm sort of glow to see him get lovingly bullied by Eileen. Families were where you found them, after all.

Catie hugged herself, she was so happy. Jake had rented this theater space on her suggestion, and Danny had been thrilled to get regular work.

Jake himself had seemed buoyantly happy in a way Catie almost didn't understand — he seemed to take unexpected joy in the simplest things. And seeing him happy made her happy. It was this crazy positive reinforcement loop that just didn't seem to end.

Even most of the members of Volare had been eventually forgiving of Catie's malfeasance, following Lola's deliberate lead. Lola had been...incredible. Catie would always be grateful to her for her understanding. She only wished that Lola would show the same empathy towards Roman.

That...was the one thing. The consequences of Roman's unmasking as Brazzer's real source were still unfolding, and mostly Roman and Lola were taking the hit. They both seemed miserable. Their pallor was beginning to spread to Volare as a whole, and even casual club members were beginning to feel it.

Which was why Catie *very* much hoped she'd done the right thing.

"So how's it coming along?" Lola said. She'd come to see the theater space at Catie's invitation, and brought two hot ciders — Catie's favorite — as well.

Catie hadn't mentioned that she'd extended more than one invitation.

"It's...coming," Catie said, smiling over the sweet smelling steam as Danny rubbed his eyes dramatically. Eileen laughed and swatted him on the arm.

"Know what they're doing yet?" Lola grinned.

"They're going to start with a bunch of

Shakespeare," Catie said. "The comedies. I figured…"

"Of course," Lola laughed. "Jake will love it."

Catie hoped so. Jake seemed to have found a new appreciation for the plays and, especially, the sonnets. Catie was in danger of getting lost in thoughts of Jake again when she caught Lola looking at her with that patented Lola concerned look.

"What?" Catie said.

"How goes it with your family?"

"Ah, yeah." Catie smiled again, this time a little sadly. All the luck in the world couldn't make some things right, but it certainly made them easier. "Jake and I go out to see Nana on the weekends, and he's making preparations so we can go out there long term when the time comes. And my dad…" She shrugged.

"I heard he wants to come back?"

"He's negotiating with the state and the IRS? Somehow? I don't want to press charges or anything, but you try telling the IRS what to do."

Lola shuddered. BDSM clubs, even ones like Volare, tended to be wary of government agencies. And the *Sizzle* article had once again raised the specter of public scrutiny by a public that wasn't always open minded where sex was concerned.

"Hey, speaking of family drama," Catie said, giving her friend a sidelong look. "You still not speaking to Roman?"

Lola punched her arm gently, and Catie wondered if Eileen-isms were contagious. "Ok, first of all, don't make it sound so juvenile. I'm *speaking* to him, just not unless I have to. And yes, I'm still extremely pissed off."

"I probably would be, too, honestly. But I feel like I have to say this: he was kinda right about me, in the end. I mean, I *know*," she said, at Lola's look. "I know, not telling you was...ok, I shouldn't get in the middle. But I feel like I have to be grateful to him for all of it. I might not have Jake if he hadn't been so..."

"Manipulative? Controlling?"

"Well...yeah."

Lola sighed. "It's not his choices that I have a problem with. I might have been completely on board if he'd given me the chance. It's that he didn't give *me* the choice. Like my opinion just didn't...matter."

"It's just, you both seem so unhappy. And I owe you both so much, and I want to see you both happy. Sucks."

"You make it sound like we were dating," Lola laughed.

Catie just shrugged, and raised an eyebrow. That thought had occurred to her before. Actually, it had occurred to everybody.

And then Catie saw him, over Lola's shoulder. She had planned to get them both here today, just to make them interact in a non-Volare context, but she hadn't intended for Roman to be so...glowering. He was definitely glowering.

"Lola," he said, advancing down the aisle of the theater, "I need to speak with you."

Catie saw Lola close her eyes, and winced.

"Lola," he said again, coming up by her elbow. Lola didn't turn to him.

"You didn't need to speak to me when you were

making decisions that could have affected all of us. I highly, highly doubt that you suddenly need to speak to me now."

Oh, shit. This was not what Catie had envisioned. At all.

"I'm just…gonna go…" Catie had never been great at gracefully backing out of anything, and it was pretty hard to tear herself away from this, even as she tried to walk away. Luckily, neither of them paid the least bit of attention.

"Well, you are wrong," Roman said.

Lola laughed, though she didn't seem happy, and finally looked at him. "You sure know how to win a girl over, Roman."

A flash of anger passed over Roman's face, the first time Catie had seen anything actually get to him. "It is excellent that you think so, Lola. It will make it easier when you are my wife."

Unfortunately, the theater had excellent acoustics. Roman's voice carried over a lull in Danny and Eileen's arguing, and slowly all focus seemed to shift to Roman and Lola, who were still glaring at each other. Lola blinked, and eventually managed to close her mouth.

"Your *what?*" she said.

Catie probably would have stayed right there, frozen to the spot, staring in just as much shock as Lola, if Jake hadn't grabbed her by the arm and led her back to the office.

"Did you *hear* that?" she said.

Jake shrugged. "It's Volare business. Something to do with licenses. I am trying to help, but in the meantime…"

"I mean, *holy crap*," Catie said. "They have to get

married?"

"I know," Jake said, and this time he couldn't suppress a grin. He had a mischievous side that Catie was just beginning to discover. She loved it. Now he lowered his eyes and said, "I'll tell you all about. Afterwards."

"After what?" Catie asked, but she was hoping she knew.

Jake hustled her into the warren-like offices, and shut the door behind him. He looked at her, and stopped. His expression changed, playfulness replaced by that look of disbelieving wonder she was getting to know, and she couldn't help herself. She darted forward to kiss him.

When they finally separated, he said, "That does not change anything, you know."

"Oh?"

"No," he said. "Today is still Friday."

Catie smiled into his chest. She knew it was Friday. It had given her an opportunity to be deliberately...disobedient.

"And suppose I'm not wearing them...?" she said, her words muffled.

His grip tightened, and Catie felt a now familiar thrill as she heard him chuckle. "Then that means I need to get you home as soon as possible," he said. "For discipline."

It was exactly what she wanted to hear.

THE END...

...But Roman and Lola's story, *Marrying the Master*, is next! Look for it in April 2013, or you can sign up for my new releases list at chloecoxwrites.com and

I'll send you a link as soon as it comes out. And if you haven't already, check out the other Club Volare books, *Sold to the Sheikh* and *Tied to the Tycoon.*

A note from the author...

Hi! Thank you so much for reading *Disciplined by the Dom*. I hope you enjoyed Jake and Catie's story, and that it brought you a bit of happiness. If you liked it, I hope you'll share it with friends you think might like it, too.

And I'd love to hear your thoughts on *Disciplined by the Dom*! You can connect with me on Facebook or email me at chloecoxwrites@gmail.com, or leave a review on Amazon or on Goodreads. I sincerely appreciate every review — I think they help other readers out, and I learn something with every review, too.

'Till the next book!

Chloe

Made in the USA
San Bernardino, CA
04 September 2013